'Has it ever occurred to you, Lanie Smith, that you have the same effect on me?'

All she could do was stare at him.

He took another step, close enough now to touch.

'I—' she began. But she really had no idea what to say. Her instinct was to deny—to shake her head and tell him that he was wrong, that this was unfair, that he didn't really mean that.

But would she actually believe what she was saying?

Did she *really* believe that incredible kiss at the Night Market had been so one-sided? Or that their daily meetings at the beach were solely between work colleagues—or, at a stretch, friends?

Or was it more that she hadn't wanted to acknowledge what was going on? That she didn't want to allow herself to consider—or hope—it was something more?

'What are we doing?' she managed eventually. 'What *is* this?'

Gray's lips quirked upwards. 'I have absolutely no idea. But right now I'd really like to kiss you.'

Dear Reader

I always find people who are really brilliant at something endlessly interesting. It doesn't matter what that something is—anything from art to sport—but I love to hear their story. Of course I'm certainly not alone in this fascination—read any newspaper or magazine and it's full of just those types of stories.

But what about all those people who are *almost* brilliant? We hear about the most famous, the real superstars of the world—but how about the guy who gets knocked out in the first round of every Grand Slam? Or the actress who finally makes it in Hollywood but never lands a leading role? These people are the very best at what they do—better than the vast majority of the population—but *still* not quite good enough.

This is where Lanie Smith comes from. She has an amazing drive and determination that has taken her all the way to international swimming championships, but in her mind she is a failure. She is *almost* brilliant. I just had to get to know her better. And I definitely needed to give her a happy-ever-after—even if she doesn't see it coming when she first meets my rather grumpy hero Grayson Manning!

I hope you enjoy Lanie and Gray's story! I love hearing from readers (really!), so please feel free to contact me via my website: www.leah-ashton.com, or e-mail me at leah@leah-ashton.com

Leah Ashton

BEWARE
OF THE BOSS

BY
LEAH ASHTON

First published in Great Britain 2013
by Mills & Boon, an imprint of Harlequin (UK) Limited.
Harlequin (UK) Limited, Eton House, 18-24 Paradise Road,
Richmond, Surrey TW9 1SR

© Leah Ashton 2013

ISBN: 978 0 263 23603 3

Harlequin (UK) policy is to use papers that are natural, renewable and recyclable products and made from wood grown in sustainable forests. The logging and manufacturing process conform to the legal environmental regulations of the country of origin.

An unashamed fan of all things happily-ever-after, **Leah Ashton** has been a lifelong reader of romance. Writing came a little bit later—although in hindsight she's been dreaming up stories for as long as she can remember. Sadly, the most popular boy in school never did suddenly fall head over heels in love with her…

Now she lives in Perth, Western Australia, with her own real-life hero, two gorgeous dogs and the world's smartest cat. By day she works in IT-land; by night she considers herself incredibly lucky to be writing the type of books she loves to read and to have the opportunity to share her own characters' happily-ever-afters with readers.

You can visit Leah at www.leah-ashton.com

This and other titles by Leah Ashton
are available in eBook format—
check out www.millsandboon.co.uk

For Isla.
Welcome to the world, honeybun!

CHAPTER ONE

WITH A GASP, Lanie Smith sat up abruptly, her floppy straw hat dislodging onto her lap and her towel a tangle amongst her hastily rearranged legs.

What on earth?

A shockingly cold nose pressing insistently against her knee answered that question. The large dog, its long red coat soaked in salt water and decorated generously with beach sand, nudged her leg, then flicked its liquid chocolate gaze hopefully in her direction.

'You lose something, buddy?'

Lanie leant forward, searching amongst the folds of her towel. The dog found its soggy-looking target first and snatched the ball up, backing a quick handful of steps away before going still and staring at her again.

'You want me to throw it?'

Knowing there was really only one answer to that question, Lanie pressed her hands into the sand and climbed to her feet. She shook her head a little, still fuzzy from her impromptu nap.

One minute she'd been reading her paperback...the next... She glanced up at the sky, looking for the sun, and breathed a silent sigh of relief when she realised it was still low and behind her. At least she hadn't slept for long.

Not that sleeping the day away would have been such a disaster. It wasn't as if she had a million other things to do.

The dog came closer and dropped the ball with a dull plop at her feet.

Hurry up.

Lanie couldn't help but smile.

'Okay, okay, buddy—here we go.'

With barely a grimace as her fingers wrapped around the slobbery ball—there was enough water here at North Cottesloe beach to wash her hands, after all—Lanie weighed up her throwing options. Back towards the water, from where the dog had obviously come? Or along the shore…?

'Luther!'

The deep voice stilled Lanie's movements. The dog momentarily glanced in the direction of the obviously familiar voice before refocussing his rapt attention on the ball.

A man loped across the blinding white sand towards her. He was shirtless, wearing only baggy, low-slung board shorts and a pair of jet-black sunglasses. The morning sun reflected off toned olive skin that glowed with exertion, and he ran a hand through slightly too long dark brown hair as he approached, leaving it standing in a haphazard arrangement.

Lanie found herself patting uselessly at her own brownish hair—which, in contrast, she was sure had *not* been rakishly enhanced by the combined effects of sand, wind and the fact that she'd done no more than loop it into half a ponytail before walking out of the house this morning.

'*Luther!*' the man said again.

The dog moved not a muscle, every line of his body focussed on Lanie's hand.

For the first time the man glanced in her direction.

And it *was* only a glance—as brief and uninterested as Luther's when he'd heard his owner call his name.

'Are you planning on keeping his ball?' the man asked, shifting his weight from foot to foot as he waited for her response.

Lanie blinked behind her own sunglasses. 'Pardon me?'

He sighed, twisting his wrist to look at his watch. 'Can you please give Luther his ball? Soonish would be great.'

The ball dropped from Lanie's fingers, but the big red dog pounced as excitedly as if she'd thrown it miles away. Now he crossed the short distance to his owner, and moments later the ball was whizzing through the air and into the shallow waves. The dog followed with huge, galumphing, splashing strides.

The man left too, without a backward glance, jogging the exact parallel distance from the lapping waves as he did every single morning.

'You're welcome,' Lanie said to his rapidly retreating broad shoulders.

What a jerk.

She knelt to stuff her towel and book into her canvas tote bag, and covered her windblown hair with her hat.

Well, at least now she knew.

In the past weeks she'd come to recognise most of the early-morning regulars at the beach—the dedicated open water swimmers who swam at seven a.m. every day, come rain, hail or shine. The walkers—both the walking-for-exercise and the walking-because-the-beach-is-gorgeous types. The joggers, the surfers, the sunbathers—and of course the dogs.

That man was also a regular. Unlike the others, who would greet Lanie with a familiar nod or smile each morning, this man appeared to be absorbed completely in his own world. He went for his run, his dog zipping about the shore in his wake—and then he left. That was it.

Dark and interesting, Lanie had thought whenever she'd seen him. *Private. Intense.*

Gorgeous. Obviously.

She wouldn't have been human not to wonder about a man like that. What did he do? What was his name? Was he married?

Not that she'd harboured any ridiculous daydreams. Lanie was, if nothing else, pragmatic.

But still—she'd wondered.

And now she had the only answer she needed. So, what was he like? *Rude*. Definitely.

Oh, well. No great loss—he could still add to her beautiful view each morning. A personality deficiency wouldn't impact on that.

With her shoes dangling from her fingers, Lanie followed a path through the green scrub-tufted dunes towards Marine Parade. Small white shells mixed amongst the sand dug into the soles of her feet. When she hit the footpath she dropped her shoes to the ground so she could step into them. The concrete was surprisingly warm, despite the lukewarm winter day.

It was Tuesday, so the Norfolk-pine-lined street was mostly empty, not crammed with cars fighting for every available space as was typical throughout summer weekends. Across the road, multi-million-dollar homes faced the cerulean ocean, with a single café nestled amongst their architecturally designed glory. The café's white-painted tables and chairs spilled outside, protected by brightly covered shade cloth sails and decorated with blue glass bottles filled with yellow daisies. Lanie's house was a two-minute walk up the hill—but a wave from the grey-haired man amongst the empty tables drew her attention.

'Lanie!' he called out, pausing his energetic sweeping to prop himself against a broom. 'Morning! Did you swim today?'

She smiled as she shook her head. 'Not today.'

'Tomorrow?'

They followed this script every day. 'Maybe.'

The man grumbled something non-distinct, but his opinion was still crystal-clear.

'Tell me what you *really* think, Bob,' she said dryly.

'Such a waste,' he said—just as he had yesterday—then patted one of the table tops. 'Coffee?'

Lanie nodded. Along with her early-morning beach visits, coffee at the eponymous Bob's Café had become part of her daily routine.

She slid onto the wooden chair, careful to avoid Bob's scruffy-looking apricot poodle who slept, oblivious, at her feet. Bob didn't wait to take her order, just shuffled inside to brew her 'usual': flat white, no sugar, extra shot of coffee.

On the table was today's newspaper, and automatically Lanie flipped it over as she waited.

A giant colour photograph almost filled the back page: a familiar, perfect, blinding white smile; slicked back, damp blond hair and eyes identical to those she saw in the mirror each day—except Sienna's were a sparkling azure blue, not brown.

'Hazel,' her mum always said. *'Not brown. If you only made more of them, Lanie, they'd be your best feature.'*

'Another gold medal,' Bob said, sliding a large mug and saucer onto the table.

Lanie shrugged. 'I know. She's doing really well. This is a great meet for her.'

Meet. Quite the understatement.

Bob raised his white-flecked eyebrows.

'I mean it,' Lanie said—and she did. 'I'm thrilled for her. Very proud of her.'

Her sister was in London, living Lanie's dream.

No, *Sienna's* dream. Lanie's dream had ended months ago, at the selection trials.

Lanie held her mug in her hands for a few moments, then raised an eyebrow at Bob, who still hovered.

'It's the relay tonight,' Bob said.

'Uh-huh.' Lanie took a too-quick sip and the hot liquid stung the roof of her mouth. She pressed her tongue against the slight pain, dismissing it.

Bob didn't push, but she felt the occasional weight of his gaze as he swept around her. He was a sports nut—pure and simple. Fanatical, actually—he had to be to have recognised her that first morning she'd emerged from her mother's house. *Lanie Smith* was far, far from a household name. *Sienna Smith*—well, that was another story. A story that could be read in the sports pages, in gushing women's magazines, or even in lads' mags accompanied by pictures of her in far more revealing bathers than her sister wore at swim-meets.

It didn't bother her. Her younger sister was suited to the limelight and she deserved it. Lanie was much happier in the shadows and perfectly satisfied with her accomplishments as a world-class relay swimmer. Besides, she certainly didn't crave the adulation that Sienna seemed to draw like a magnet.

Mostly satisfied. Lanie mentally corrected herself. *Mostly satisfied with her accomplishments.*

Absently she flicked through the sporting pages, full of photos of winners on podiums.

'Wish it was you?'

She hadn't realised Bob had approached her table again, and she glanced up in surprise. 'Of course not,' Lanie replied—snapped, really. Immediately she wished she could swallow the words. 'I'm retired,' she clarified, more calmly.

He nodded and drifted politely away again—but Lanie didn't miss the questions, and maybe concern, in his eyes.

She stood and left a handful of coins on the table, trying to ignore how her eyes had started to tingle and squint.

It was the sea breeze.

She slung her bag onto her shoulder and took big, brisk strides to exit the café and get home as quickly as possible.

She'd walked past three huge mansions, heading towards the street where her mother's small neat cottage was, when something caught her eye.

The glint of sun off a sweaty, perfectly muscled chest.

That man.

He jogged along the footpath on the opposite side of the road. His dog was now on a lead, intermittently gazing up at his owner in adoration.

Lanie felt herself tense, for no reason she could fathom.

She'd slowed her walk, but now she deliberately sped up—back to the pace she'd been before.

She didn't care about that guy. Didn't care if he was rude. Didn't care what he thought of her.

Didn't care what Bob thought.

Didn't care what her sister thought. Didn't care what anyone thought.

She held her head high and walked briskly past. With purpose.

But out of the corner of her eye she couldn't help but watch the man.

And notice that he paid her absolutely no attention at all.

It was as if she were invisible.

The knock on Lanie's front door later that night was not unexpected.

She headed down her narrow hallway, her slippers thudding against the hundred-year-old floorboards.

She flung the door open, and—as expected—behind the fly screen stood Teagan. Her long black hair was swept off her face and semi contained in a messy bun on the top of her head, and her eyes sparkled behind red-framed glasses.

Her oldest friend held up a plastic grocery bag. 'I have four types of cheese, olives, sundried tomatoes, and something I believe is called quince. The guy at the deli told me it was awesome, but I remain sceptical.'

Teagan bounded up the hall, as comfortable in this house as her own. As kids they'd split their time between their family's homes, although Teagan's family had long upgraded and moved on, while Lanie's mum had quite happily stayed put in the house she'd grown up in.

Lanie watched as Teagan pottered around the kitchen, locating a large wooden board and helping herself to cutlery.

She didn't bother asking why her friend was here as it was so obvious. Equally obvious was the fact that Teagan had ignored her when she'd politely declined her offer to hang out with her tonight.

'It's just another race, Teags,' she'd told her. *'I'll be fine.'*

Apparently she'd convinced Teagan about as well as she'd convinced herself.

Soon they'd settled on the rug in front of the TV, red wine in hand, cheese platter set out in front of them.

'You *do* know the final isn't until, like, two a.m.?' Lanie asked, her legs sprawled out in front of her.

'That's what coffee is for,' Teagan said between sips of wine. 'Besides, this current job I could do in my sleep. Hardly anyone calls Reception. In fact I'm starting to think they don't have any customers at all. You know...' Teagan paused, leaning forward conspiratorially. 'I reckon it's possible that it's all an elaborate front for something dodgy. I've always thought that my boss has shifty eyes...'

Lanie laughed out loud as Teagan outlined a typically outlandish theory. More than once Lanie had suspected that Teagan's preference for temping over a more permanent job was purely to get new material—whether they caught up for coffee, dinner or a drink, it was guaranteed that her friend would have a new story to tell.

As they ate—and polished off the bottle of wine—Lanie flicked from channel to channel of the sports coverage—heats of rowing, horses leaping over huge fences across country, cyclists whizzing around a velodrome.

'So, have you made a decision?' Teagan said a while later, her tone much more careful than before.

Lanie shifted uncomfortably. 'Has my mother been in touch?'

Teagan pulled a face. 'God, no. And it isn't like your mum's not capable of nagging you directly.'

Lanie's lips quirked unevenly.

Teagan drew her legs up so she sat cross-legged. '*I* was just wondering.' She paused. 'Worrying, maybe,' she added softly.

Lanie found herself biting the inside of her lip. When it happened twice in one day—first Bob, and now her best friend—that look really couldn't be misinterpreted.

They felt sorry for her.

Her whole focus had been aimed in one direction for so long. But now the pool wasn't calling her to training each morning. Her coach wasn't yelling at her. Her times weren't creeping down—or up. She didn't have another meet to aim for.

She had no goals.

Even though she wasn't the slightest bit hungry she reached for the cheese platter, busying herself with slicing bread and cheese and then taking her time to chew and swallow, not looking at Teagan

She mentally pulled herself into shape.

'I've decided not to go back to my old job,' she said, finally answering the question. 'It's time for a change. Managing the swim school is too much the same thing I've been doing for ever.' She attempted a carefree laugh. 'Although I can't imagine a job where my office doesn't smell of chlorine!'

Teagan, ever the good friend, smiled back, but she wasn't about to let her off the hook. 'So, the new plan is…?'

On the TV a rider toppled off his horse when the big grey animal slid to a stop before a hulking log fence. Lanie watched as he immediately jumped to his feet. She could see what he was telling everyone with his body language—*I'm fine!*—but the commentator was explaining in a clipped British accent that this meant he was disqualified. His dream was over.

The man patted his horse's neck, then leant forward until his silk-covered helmet rested against the horse's cheek.

Lanie knew *exactly* how he felt.

'I don't know—maybe I'll finish my business degree,' she said with a shrug. Three-quarters finished years ago, she'd abandoned it leading up to the national titles, intending to defer only for a semester or two. But then she'd made the Australian team, and everything had changed.

'Still living here?' Teagan's wrinkled nose conveyed exactly what she thought of that idea.

Lanie didn't know. She'd moved back in months earlier, after the selection trials. At the time it had seemed sensible—she'd taken extended leave from her job, needed a break from swimming entirely, and without an income she couldn't afford the rent on her little one-bedder in Scarborough without putting a huge dent into the savings she had earmarked for a house deposit. Her mum and sister had been focused on Sienna—not unusual in itself—so she'd reasoned that it wouldn't be too bad.

But they'd both be back soon.

'Maybe.'

Teagan raised an eyebrow. 'Hmm. You're always welcome to crash at mine. Or I can put a good word in for you at my temp agency?'

'And I can inadvertently work for an international drug cartel?' she asked with a smile.

Teagan stuck her tongue out at her.

So the conversation was over—for now.

Some time during one of the rowing finals Lanie noticed Teagan had fallen asleep sprawled against the front of her sofa. She padded over to extract the empty wine glass from her friend's hand, and then took her time washing up and tidying the kitchen.

She wasn't at all tired. Quite the opposite. In fact with every passing minute she felt more alert, more awake.

Before Teagan had arrived she'd considered not watching

the race at all. She'd told herself that it wasn't as if anyone would know—and she'd find out the result tomorrow, anyway.

But she hadn't really believed she could do that, and now she *knew* she couldn't. It wasn't quite the same, but she recognised how she was feeling: as if *she* was racing today.

The anticipation, the adrenalin, the nervous energy. Muted, but there.

From her kitchen bench Lanie watched the swimmers walk out for the men's hundred-metre breaststroke final. Watched them stretch and roll their shoulders, wiggle their legs about.

Then she watched the race—listened to the crowd, to the increasing hysteria of the commentators, and then watched the moment the winner won gold.

Automatically she smiled in reaction to the winner's smile, and then grinned to herself when she realised what she'd done.

See? She could do this. Tonight was just like any other night in front of the television. She'd watched her sister win two medals and been genuinely nervous and then over the moon for her. If she was going to have regrets, or be overwhelmed by jealousy or resentment or something equally unpleasant and inappropriate, she would have done it by now.

It really was just another race.

On the screen, groups of swimmers began to walk out to the pool. Sweden, in their uniform of vivid blue and gold. Japan, with all four women holding hands as they waved to the crowd. The Dutch in orange and grey.

And then the Australian team.

'Lanie?' Teagan poked her head over the top of the couch and blinked sleepy eyes in her direction.

'Perfect timing!' Lanie said, managing to sound remarkably normal. 'The race is just about to start.'

Her friend raised an eyebrow.

Okay. Maybe she didn't sound totally normal. But surely a little bit of tension was to be expected?

The swimmers had all discarded their tracksuits and onto

the blocks stepped the lead-out swimmer. Australia was in lane four, sandwiched between the United States and the Netherlands.

Teagan's eyes were glued to the television when Lanie sat beside her, but her friend still managed to reach out and grab her hand. She shot a short glance in Lanie's direction as she squeezed it—hard.

'You okay?'

Lanie nodded. 'Totally.'

'Take your marks.'

Pause.

Complete silence.

BEEP!

And they were off.

The first leg was good—strong. The United States touched first, but there was nothing in it. By the end of the second lap Australia had drawn level.

Then the third Aussie girl dived in, sluicing through the water like an arrow.

This was *her* leg. The girl was just like her—the fastest of the heat swimmers, awarded with the final relay berth amongst the more elite girls.

She was doing a brilliant job. Holding her own.

Would Lanie have?

She closed her eyes, squeezing them shut tight.

She imagined herself in the water. Remembered the way her focus became so narrow, so all-encompassing, that she didn't hear the crowd—didn't hear a thing. It was just her body and the water, and all she could control was her technique.

Stroke, stroke, *breathe.* Stroke, stroke...

The crowd—a world away—was suddenly much louder, and Lanie's eyes popped open. The anchor swimmer was in the water, and Great Britain had a chance for a medal. The crowd had gone wild.

Teagan squeezed her hand again, harder, and Lanie blinked, refocussing her attention.

Australia had pulled ahead. They were going to win.

And just like that—they had.

The girls had done it, and done it in style—in record time. They deserved every accolade the over-excited commentator was bestowing upon them.

They filled the television screen, swim caps stripped off, damp hair long around their shoulders, as they completed the standard pool-side interview.

'Lanie?' Teagan's voice was full of concern.

Despite her own mental reassurances that she was fine, and the many times she'd told herself she was a bigger person than to be jealous or resentful or whatever, she suddenly realised she wasn't.

A tear splashed onto her hands, and she looked down to where her fingers were knotted in the flannelette of her pyjamas.

She'd been wallowing. Treading water until this moment—waiting for tonight, for this race.

Why?

Because tonight was the end. The end of her swimming dream.

Teagan silently shoved a handful of tissues in front of her and Lanie dabbed at her cheeks. Blew her nose. And considered what to do next.

She needed to do something—anything. And she had to do it *now*. She couldn't wake up tomorrow and be the also-ran swimmer.

She turned to face Teagan on the couch. Her friend was so close to be as good as shoulder to shoulder with her, but she'd wisely not made a move to comfort her.

'I need a job,' Lanie said.

Teagan's eyes widened, but then she smiled. 'But no drug cartels?'

'Or anything involving swimming.'

Her friend's smile broadened. 'Consider it done.'

CHAPTER TWO

GRAYSON MANNING SHOVED his chair away from his desk, then covered the generous space between the desk and the door in quick, agitated strides.

Outside his office, his assistant's desk was empty.

He glanced at his watch, confused. It was well after nine a.m., and Rodney was always on time. Gray insisted upon it.

He frowned as he walked into the hallway. Thankfully a woman sat behind the glossy white reception desk. Behind her, 'Manning' was spelt out in ridiculously large chrome block capitals.

What was her name again? Cathy? Katie?

'Caroline,' she said, unprompted, as he approached—reminding him he'd guessed wrong last time he'd asked her a question, too.

'Caroline,' he repeated. He'd been told doing so was useful when remembering names—not that it had helped him so far. 'Where's Rodney?'

The woman blinked. Then bit her lip, glancing away for a moment. 'Um…Mr Manning, Rodney resigned…' A pause. 'Yesterday.'

Gray's jaw clenched. 'Our agreement with the agency specifies at least two weeks' notice must be provided.'

The woman nodded, her blond ponytail bouncing in agreement. 'I believe he asked your permission that his resignation be effective immediately.'

'I didn't agree to that.'

Caroline's lips twitched. 'I'm pretty sure you did. Rodney forwarded me your e-mail so he could organise cancellation of his building access and so on. It was there in writing.'

Gray pulled his phone from his jacket pocket and quickly scrolled through yesterday's sent messages. Yesterday had been stupidly busy—back-to-back meetings, a major issue with one of his contractors, and a lead on a new investment opportunity in South East Asia.

Even so, surely he would have noticed if... *Letter of Resignation.*

It wasn't even a vague subject line. He really needed to start paying more attention to his inbox. But then, that was one of the reasons why he had an assistant: to prioritise his mail, to nag him to respond to anything important, and to allow him to pay no attention to anything that wasn't.

The irony was not lost on him.

Without another word he headed up the hallway to the opposite end of the floor. To his father's office.

A mirror image of his own, Gordon Manning's office also had a smaller adjacent waiting area—although his was complete with an actual assistant.

'Marilyn—'

Unlike Caroline, the older lady didn't even attempt to hide her smile. She shook her head. 'Gray, Gray, Gray...'

'I need a new assistant.'

'So I hear.'

His lips thinned. 'Does everyone but me know that Rodney resigned?'

'A group of us had farewell drinks last night. Lovely guy.'

'I was unaware you were so close,' he replied dryly. 'He was only here a couple of weeks.'

'Two months,' Marilyn corrected smoothly.

Really? Since his father had announced his impending retirement six months ago, Gray could barely remember what day it was. He was working seven days a week, and easily twelve-hour days.

'Is my father in?'

'No, not today.'

His father hadn't been into the office in months. Initially his transition to retirement had been gradual—and Gray had been unsure if his father was capable of retiring at all. But soon Gordon's days in the office had been reduced to only a few hours, and then to nothing. And while Marilyn continued to manage his dad's life, now she did so exclusively via e-mail.

A month ago Gordon Manning had had his no-expense-spared retirement party and that had made it all official. But Gray wasn't silly enough to clear out his dad's office just yet—apart from the fact it contained about forty years' worth of god-knew-what paperwork, it would be a while before Gordon—or Gray, come to think of it—could imagine a Manning Developments office without a desk for its founder.

'So you can help me today? Fantastic. I need you to accompany me to a meeting in West Perth. And to sort out my flights for next week. And—'

But Marilyn was shaking her head. 'No need. Your new assistant should be here soon.'

Oh. The agency must already be on to it. Even so…

'I'd rather not have someone completely new to Manning with me today. This is a very important meeting. It's essential that—'

Marilyn's look froze him mid-sentence, exactly as it had frozen him many times before—although the vast majority of such glares had been twenty-five years ago. A kid learnt quickly *not* to mess with Marilyn.

'If you don't want a new assistant, be nice to the assistant you have.'

'I *am* nice.'

Her eyebrows rose right up beneath her dead straight fringe.

'Be nice to this one, Gray. Let's try for three months, this time, hey?'

* * *

Almost an hour later, Caroline ushered Gray's new assistant into his office.

'Mr Manning?'

He was just finishing an e-mail, so he barely glanced in the direction of the figure in his doorway and instead just waved an arm in the general vicinity of one of the soft leather chairs in front of his desk.

Absently, he heard the door thud quietly shut, and then the click of heels on the marble floor—but all his attention was on the e-mail he was composing:

I look forward to discussing the proposal further...

No. He hit the delete key half a dozen times, maybe a little harder than was necessary. He didn't want any discussion. He wanted a decision. The deal was already behind schedule. He needed a *yes* and he needed it last week.

I trust you'll agree...

That was even worse. He held down the delete key again, thinking.

But that was the problem. He was thinking too much. It was just an e-mail—an e-mail to an investment partner with whom he already had an excellent rapport. The proposal was little more than a formality.

Or at least it should be. But their last meeting had been... *off*. It had been subtle—more questions than he'd normally expect, more careful perusal of the numbers Gray had shown him. All perfectly normal things for a wise investor to do. The thing was that *this* particular investor had so much confidence in Manning that he was usually rather relaxed about conducting his own due diligence.

Quite simply—he'd trusted Manning.

But now...

Maybe it was a coincidence that this new-found caution coincided with Gray's father's retirement...

Gray didn't believe that for a second.

And it was damned infuriating.

Gray glanced up. His eyes landed on the woman's hands—long, elegant fingers, unpainted, neat, short tips. She was sluggishly rubbing each hand down her thighs, the movement slow but clearly triggered by nerves.

She wore trousers, not a skirt, he noticed.

'How do I finish this e-mail?' he asked. His tone was sharper than he'd intended, and Marilyn's words echoed momentarily.

His gaze shot to the woman's face.

As their eyes met her body gave a little jolt and she gasped—quite loudly.

Immediately one of those long-fingered hands was slapped to her mouth.

Her eyes widened as she looked at him.

And they were very lovely eyes, he acknowledged. Big and brown, framed by dark lashes—even though he was almost certain she wore no make-up. They watched him with unexpected intensity and an expression that was impossible to read.

He didn't understand. Surely his request wasn't so shocking? Abrupt, maybe, but hardly earth-shattering.

When the silence continued he shrugged, his temporary interest in her reaction rapidly morphing into frustration.

He didn't have time for this. The agency would just have to send someone else.

'I don't think this is going to work out,' he said, very evenly. 'Thanks for your time.'

He didn't bother to wait for her to leave, just gritted his teeth and got back to his e-mail.

Again he only half listened to the sound of her heels on the marble—although soon he realised she was coming closer, not going further away.

'Regards,' she said, from right behind his shoulder.

'What?'

He looked up at her. She was somehow bigger than he'd expected—taller, and wider through the shoulders. She leant forward slightly as she studied his computer, her long hair shining in the sunlight that flooded through the office's floor-to-ceiling windows.

'I'd delete all that stuff at the end, and just say *Regards*. Or *Sincerely*. Or however you normally sign off your e-mails.' She met his eyes, and this time she didn't look like a deer caught in the headlights. She watched him steadily, and there was a sharpness to her gaze that he appreciated.

Her eyes were definitely hazel, he realised. Not brown.

When he didn't say anything, she explained further. 'Judging by the e-mail trail beneath this one, you've been having this conversation for a while.'

Gray nodded.

'And you want a resolution? But you don't want to be seen as pushy?'

'Exactly,' he said, surprised.

'Well, then,' she said, as if it was the most obvious thing in the world. 'Sometimes saying less is more.'

She straightened up and took a step away from his chair.

Silently, he deleted his half-written sentence, ended the e-mail as she'd suggested, then hit *'Send.'*

Good. It was gone.

He stood, and with this action, the woman took another rapid step away. Then she rolled her shoulders back, and thrust out her hand.

'Elaine Smith,' she said, very crisply. 'Lanie.'

Automatically he grasped her hand. It was cool and delicate. And she *was* tall. But even in heels she was an inch shorter than him.

Her suit jacket was a dark grey and a little tight across the chest—and her soft pink shirt wasn't sitting quite right, with one side of her collar higher than the other. Combined with her loose, wavy hair and lack of discernible make-up, no one would call her perfectly presented.

He would call her pretty, though. Very pretty.

Gray rapidly dispatched that unexpected musing. The appearance of his employees was irrelevant. All he cared about was their ability to do their job.

And, despite her slightly odd initial reaction to him, there was an air of practicality to this woman that was appealing. Plus she'd been right about the e-mail.

Most importantly he needed an assistant, and she was here.

'I have a meeting in half an hour in West Perth.'

For a moment she looked at him blankly. 'So I have the job?'

He nodded impatiently. 'Yes, of course.'

A beat passed.

He sighed. 'Anything else?'

'Oh,' she said. 'No.'

He turned back to his computer and a moment later she walked away, her heels again clicking loudly.

He briefly wondered if she needed help figuring out how to log into her computer or anything—but then another e-mail popped in that he urgently needed to attend to, and that was that.

Surely it wasn't that difficult? She seemed smart. She'd figure it out.

Lanie almost collapsed into her new, plush leather office chair.

Her phone trilled its musical message notification from within the depths of her bag, but for now she ignored it.

Of course she'd forgotten to put it onto silent mode prior to her interview.

Thank goodness she hadn't received that message a few minutes earlier. She could just about imagine Grayson Manning's reaction to *that*.

But then would that have been such a bad thing?

If he'd stuck with his original conclusion—that she wasn't suitable—she'd have walked out of this office no worse than how she'd walked in: without a job.

With the added benefit of *not* working for Mr Grumpy Pants.

No. Not a bad thing at all.

And yet she'd had her chance to leave. She had her chance still to walk away. No one would force her to stay. Not even the employment agency she was working for.

Which reminded her…

Lanie fished out her phone. As expected, the waiting message was from Teagan. As she'd been whisked up to the twenty-fifth floor in a seriously shiny mirrored lift she'd tapped out an urgent message to her friend:

What did you do??!

Because this building was definitely not what Lanie had been expecting of her first assignment with the agency. Yes, she'd known the role was as a personal assistant, but after seven years managing the swim school she'd been unconvinced she really had the skills for such a role—but Teagan had been adamant. *'You'll be fine,'* she'd said. *'Piece of cake,'* she'd said.

Given her lack of relevant experience, Lanie had imagined she'd be working somewhere small. Somewhere that couldn't afford a true executive assistant. Somewhere she could kind of figure it all out as she went along.

Manning Developments was *not* that place.

Teagan's text message therefore did not surprise her at all.

I spruced up your CV. Just a little.

Right.

Lanie rolled her head backwards until it rested on the high back of her chair and stared up at the ceiling.

The sensible thing to do would be to leave. She didn't have the experience for a role like this, and if she stuffed it up then the agency, Teagan *and* herself would all look pretty bad.

It was sweet of Teagan—annoying, inappropriate, and dishonest—but sweet.

It should end here.

But she remained at her vast new desk. For the same reason she'd stayed in Grayson's office after she'd recognised him as the man from the beach.

For long seconds she'd searched for the cutting comments he deserved after his performance at the beach—but then, before she'd gathered her thoughts, she'd realised he'd just *dismissed* her.

Again. Just as he had at the beach, he'd carried on as if she was irrelevant to his world. Why on earth would she want to work for someone who would treat her like that?

But she couldn't let that man—*Grayson*—ignore her again.

So here she was. With a job she didn't really want, working for a man she didn't like.

Lanie wiggled the wireless mouse on the desk and the large flatscreen monitor blinked instantly to life, revealing a login screen.

Her gaze flicked to the still open door to Grayson's office, but then immediately away. That he would be of no help at all was obvious.

She stood and headed for the hallway—Caroline, the little plaque on the reception desk had proclaimed. She should be able to point her in the direction of IT Support or something.

She could do this. It couldn't be too difficult.

She'd figure out *why* she was doing it later.

CHAPTER THREE

THE LITTLE GREEN man started blinking, so with a coffee cup gripped firmly in each hand Lanie made her way across a very busy St Georges Terrace.

'Lanie!'

A fierce breeze whipped between the high-rise buildings, blowing her loose hair every which way and partially covering her eyes. Not that she needed a visual aid to identify that particular deep and demanding voice.

Calmly she stepped onto the footpath and Grayson met her halfway, jogging down his building's steps and deftly negotiating the sea of lunchtime pedestrian traffic.

'We're going to be late,' he said. 'Why didn't you say something?'

Lanie tossed her hair out of her face and met his gaze as she handed him his triple-shot latte.

'I did mention that there may not be time for a coffee.'

Grayson blinked. As always, he seemed genuinely surprised. 'Oh...' he said.

In the week she'd worked for him this routine had already become familiar. He was rather like a mad scientist—so utterly focussed on his work that the practicalities of life seemed beyond him.

It would have been endearing—except...

'Well, make sure it doesn't happen again.'

Lanie bit her lip.

Remember the money. Remember the money...

It was the money, Lanie had decided. The reason she hadn't already quit.

Thanks to Teagan's creativity with her CV, and her ability so far to fudge her way through the job, she was earning almost twice what she had at the swim school. And she needed the money so she could move out of her mother's place as soon as possible—before she and Sienna returned from Europe, preferably.

That was the only reason she was here. Nothing to do with that morning on the beach.

Lanie nodded tightly. 'I've got a car waiting for us.' She gestured with her spare hand in its direction, and to the driver idling illegally in the clearway. Grayson opened his mouth, but Lanie jumped in before he could get a word out. 'The laptop, projector and business specs are on the back seat.'

In response his eyebrows rose, just slightly. 'Good,' he said.

Again Lanie bit her lip. *How about a thank-you, huh?*

She pivoted on her heel and strode towards the car.

Remember the money. Remember the money. Remember the—

The toe of her shoe caught on something and Lanie stumbled. But before she had much time to register that the grey pavers of the footpath were rapidly becoming closer her descent was suddenly halted.

Grayson's arm was strong and solid and warm around her waist. In an effortless movement he pulled her upwards and towards him, so she was pressed against his impeccably suited body.

She tilted her chin to look up at him.

He caught her gaze—*really* caught it—and for a moment Lanie was completely speechless.

His eyes weren't just grey—they were flecked with blue. And with his face now arranged in concern, not hard with tension, he was somehow—impossibly—even more handsome.

Of course she already knew he was gorgeous. To pretend otherwise would be ridiculous. And, frustratingly, beautiful people didn't become less beautiful simply by their unlike-able behaviour.

Less *attractive*, though. They did become less attractive. He'd proved that, that day on the beach. And each day since then.

But right now Grayson did *not* seem unattractive. Right now, with the subtle scent of his aftershave and the warmth of his arm and body confusing her, he was anything but.

The side of her body he touched...no *everywhere* he touched, reacted to him. Electricity flooded through her.

'You okay?'

Because it was all she could manage, she simply nodded mutely.

He took a step away from her and amazingly she had the presence of mind not to follow him. She took a deep breath, rolled her shoulders back, and rebalanced on her own two feet.

She realised she was gripping her coffee cup hard enough to slightly crumple the cardboard, and made herself loosen her grip.

Then he smiled. It was a subtle expression—far from broad—but it was the first Grayson Manning smile she'd witnessed.

Once again her ability to form words evaporated.

He covered the short distance to the car and opened the door for her.

She slipped past him, not catching his gaze. With every moment she was increasingly aware that she *really* needed to pull herself together.

If she was going to keep working for Grayson she needed to erase completely from her subconscious even the smallest skerrick of romantic daydreams involving her boss.

Obviously the agency would not approve.

Secondly she—*Lanie*—did not approve. She might not

have extensive experience in the corporate world, but even she knew getting involved with your boss was…well, pretty dumb.

And thirdly, Grayson was not about to be overcome by lust when it came to Lanie Smith.

Lanie's lips quirked up at the idea of Grayson arriving at her front door to take her out to dinner. It was laughable.

She settled into the soft leather of the back seat as Grayson closed her door, and moments later he was sliding into the car from the opposite side.

Lanie took a good long gulp of her coffee, hoping that the addition of caffeine would help get her brain back to speed.

She fully expected Grayson to flip open his laptop as the car pulled way, or to make another one of his seemingly endless phone calls. But instead he turned towards her.

He cleared his throat, the sound unexpected and awkward in the quiet vehicle.

'Thank you for the coffee,' he said gruffly.

Lanie shot a look in his direction, not immediately sure she'd heard him correctly.

But his expression was genuine. Not quite contrite—that wouldn't be Grayson Manning—but still…

'Not a problem, Grayson.'

He nodded, then glanced away through his darkly tinted window at the passing traffic.

Without looking at her, he spoke again.

'You can call me Gray.'

The beach was near deserted the following morning. Gray's bare feet smacked rhythmically against the wet sand, his progress only occasionally punctuated with a splash when the waves stretched across his path.

Luther was well ahead of Gray, having abandoned his ball to begin enthusiastically digging a hole to China. Beyond Luther rocky fingers of coastline stretched into the ocean, and distant cranes for hoisting shipping containers formed blurry silhouettes against the sky.

It was cool—it was only July after all—and all but the most dedicated swimmers had abandoned the beach on such a dull and overcast day.

But today Gray needed to run.

Maybe he'd hoped the bite of the frigid air in his lungs would help. Or, more likely, it was that heavy ache in his legs that he craved.

Because out here he was in control. He could run as far as he wanted—further even than his body wanted to go.

And Gray liked being in control. He was used to it. Expected it.

He was in control of everything he did in both his business and his private life. He knew what he was doing and could plan with absolute confidence how things were going to work out.

By Gray's reckoning, his father's retirement should be no more than a blip on Manning's radar—after all, it had been many years since Gordon Manning had spearheaded a project. For the past five years Gray *had* been Manning's CEO in all but name. So Gordon's retirement was nothing more than a formality. Nothing would change except he'd eventually have to repurpose his dad's offices.

That was how it was supposed to be happening.

It was still how Gray thought it *should* have happened.

But it hadn't.

Things *had* changed.

That irritating e-mail from the suddenly cautious investor was just one example. Not of many—far from it—but enough to frustrate the hell out of Gray.

An extra question here or there shouldn't bother him. Or decisions taking longer than he felt they should. Or even that subtle, almost but not quite imperceptible shift in the atmosphere at meetings...

Even Gray had to smile at that. Since when had he been so sensitive to a change in *feel*?

Well, whatever it was that had changed—it *had*. And it did bother him. Because it wasn't just an irritation...all these questions and atmosphere-shifts ...it had the potential to impact his bottom line.

In fact it already was.

And Gray was *not* going to tolerate that.

In his peripheral vision, Gray noticed a lone figure walking near the dunes. As he glanced in her direction the woman waved, while her other hand firmly held an oversized floppy hat to her head.

Automatically Gray waved back, then refocussed. Deliberately he crossed from the wet sand to the dry, wanting the extra demand on his muscles the deep, soft sand forced from his body.

It turned out that, despite the many years since his dad had actually led a Manning project, for some of his clients Gordon Manning had been a very real and very important presence—somewhere behind the scenes.

The reality that it had truly been Gray they'd been working with—not Gray as Gordon's mouthpiece—didn't matter, and that exasperated Gray.

He deserved the trust he thought he'd already earned. He deserved his stature in Australia's business community.

A larger wave pushed far up the beach and Gray's bare feet splashed through foamy puddles as the water slid back into the ocean.

It also annoyed him that he hadn't realised this reality. That he hadn't fully understood what it meant to be Gordon Manning's son, regardless of his own track record and years of success.

So it was frustrating and exasperating and irritating...

But it was also...

Gray's time.

Now was his time to prove himself.

And nothing could be allowed to stand in his way.

Lanie dropped her arm as Gray disappeared into the distance. He'd waved each morning since she'd started at Manning, although he'd shown no sign of realising she was the woman he'd been so rude to on the beach that morning of the relay final. Now, knowing Gray, she doubted he ever would.

She'd considered telling him—but what would that achieve?

Lanie knew the answer to that: a blank stare, followed directly by a look that said *Why are you wasting my time with this?*

That was a look she was quickly becoming familiar with. At least now she didn't take it personally. Pretty much everything not immediately related to Manning and preferably relevant *right at that moment* elicited exactly that look.

'Which hotel would you like me to book for you in Adelaide?'

When he'd discovered he was not, in fact, booked into his favourite hotel, he'd booked himself in, then sent Lanie a helpful e-mail with the name of the 'correct' hotel for next time.

'For that presentation tomorrow, would you like me to include the numbers from the Jameson project?'

Turned out she'd guessed right with that one…

So a returned wave each morning was both unexpected and welcome. Although ignoring the woman he worked with every single day would have been quite a stretch—even for Gray.

With Gray and Luther little more than specks in the distance, Lanie started walking again and allowed her thoughts to circle back to where they'd been before the flash of Luther's red coat against the sand had distracted her.

It would be odd, she'd just decided, if she wasn't jealous of her sister.

Wouldn't it?

She didn't know. It was what had got her out of the house so ridiculously early on a work day. She needed the beach. The space, the salt and the sound of the waves… It was all as familiar to her as breathing.

Water had always helped her. Whether chlorinated or not, it was where she gravitated at times of stress. When her dad had left it had seemed natural. He was, after all, the reason she loved water. With an offshore mining job he'd rarely been home—but when he had he'd spent all his time at the beach.

As an adult, she looked back and wondered whether he'd simply tolerated the fact she'd clung to him like a limpet when he was home—rather than her more romanticised version in which she'd told herself she'd been his swimming buddy.

Because surely if he'd really wanted her there he would have bothered to stay in touch after he'd left. Or not left at all.

But if nothing else he'd given Lanie her love of water and the genes that helped her swim very quickly through it.

It had been a mistake to skip the beach earlier in the week. She needed to rectify it. Even today, with the wind whipping off the waves and gluing her long cargo trousers and thin woollen jumper to her skin, it was the right place for her to attempt to organise her thoughts and her reactions.

Sienna had e-mailed her overnight, full of post-championships euphoria. From the magnificence of the closing ceremony to how much fun she was having, through to how she was dealing with the rabid tabloid press after being seen out on a date with a British rower.

Lanie had seen the photos—and the headlines—as they'd made it to Australia too. *'Golden couple'. 'Winners in love'.*

Jealousy? Whatever it was she was feeling, she hadn't defined it.

Until Sienna's e-mail.

It hadn't been until right at the end, amongst all the glitz and excitement, that her sister had acknowledged how Lanie might be feeling. Her sister wasn't stupid, or heartless. A bit oblivious at times—but then, that was Sienna.

Somehow, though, Sienna's awkward attempts at making the contrast in their situations seem somehow okay had hit home harder than anything else.

How are you doing? It wasn't the same without you. You should be so proud of your personal best, though. Any other year you definitely would've made the team.

And so here she was, at the beach.

Walking today, not swimming—but the scale and scope of the ocean helped, just as she'd known it would.

She envied Sienna. She *was* jealous.

Today she allowed herself to be.

CHAPTER FOUR

THE UNEXPECTED SENSATION of warmth against his chest snatched Gray's attention from the report he'd been reading. He glanced downwards, to discover a trail of pale brown liquid trickling in multiple rivulets down his front.

A brief perusal of the obvious culprit—the takeaway coffee cup in his hand—revealed a leak beneath the lid.

He swore. Loudly. He had a meeting right in this office in less than twenty minutes.

Tossing the defective lid into the bin beneath his desk, Gray downed the rest of his coffee as he tapped a short message into Manning's internal instant messaging system.

Moments later his office door swung open, although Lanie paused before walking in. 'You said you had a problem?' she asked.

He stood, his gaze moving downwards as he surveyed the damage to his shirt and pulled the damp fabric away from his skin. With the other hand he gestured for Lanie to come closer.

Moments later her long, efficient stride had her by his side. 'Nice one,' she said, a hint of a smile in her tone. 'I don't suppose you have a spare shirt?'

'If I did,' he said, for the first time transferring his attention from the shirt to Lanie, 'would I—?'

His eyes met hers and he momentarily had absolutely no idea what he'd been about to say.

She stood closer than he'd expected. Or maybe it was just her height. When she was in her heels they were very nearly eye to eye, and he still wasn't quite used to that sensation.

Plus today she looked…*different.*

Her hair, he realised. It was tied back. It highlighted the striking structure of her face—the defined cheekbones, the firm chin—and her skin's perfect golden glow.

He'd thought her pretty when he'd first met her, but right now she looked…

As he watched she raised an eyebrow.

Gray blinked. 'If I had a spare shirt…' he tried again '…would I need you?'

He looked down at his ruined clothing again, yanking his mind back on track. So what if he'd noticed Lanie looked nice today?

Lanie crossed her arms in front of herself. 'What size are you?' she asked.

Not for the first time she'd pre-empted his next question. 'I have no idea.'

She didn't bother to hide her sigh. 'How can you not know that?'

Gray shrugged. 'I shop in bulk. Those couple of times a year I shop, I figure out what size I am then.'

He reached for his shirt, automatically sliding button after button undone. He'd tugged it off his shoulders and gathered the fabric in his hands before he noticed Lanie had backed off a few steps and was currently staring out the window.

'This is how I normally work out my size,' he explained, finding the tag beneath the collar. 'There you go. Turns out I wear a forty-two-inch shirt.'

'And you'd like me to go buy you a replacement?'

'Exactly.'

Not meeting his eyes, Lanie turned away from the window and took a step back towards the door. 'You know, I could've just checked the tag for you. No need to…' a pause '…undress.'

For the first time Gray noticed the tinge of pink to her cheekbones. He suspected the right thing to do would be to apologise. But with the words right on the tip of his tongue he paused.

'My shirt was covered in hot coffee,' he said, instead. 'And this way you can take the shirt with you. To check the size or whatever. Here.'

He thrust the shirt out in front of him.

Now she met his gaze, and hers wasn't bashful any more. It was razor-sharp and most definitely unimpressed.

He just shrugged. He'd done too much second-guessing recently. The equation was simple—he needed a new shirt and quickly. That was it. Anyone walking down the beach most mornings in summer saw a heck of a lot more skin than he'd just revealed to his assistant.

He steadfastly ignored the subtlest echo of Marilyn's words in his head. *Be nice to this one.*

Lanie reached out and their fingers brushed as she snatched the shirt away. Gray watched as her blush spread like quick fire across her cheeks, but her gaze never wavered from his.

'Thank you,' he said.

She raised the subtlest eyebrow, but remained silent.

See? He was nice. He checked his watch. 'You've got about ten minutes.'

Gray thought he might have heard Lanie muttering something as she strode out of the room.

Something about remembering money?

'He took off his *shirt*?'

Teagan's voice was incredulous as she raised the pizza slice to her lips.

'Uh-huh,' Lanie said, rounding her kitchen bench to join

Teagan at the dining table. 'I guess it's not that big a deal. I've seen it all before at the beach.'

Teagan chewed thoughtfully for a few moments. 'You don't think he was…like…coming onto you or something?'

Lanie just about choked on her own mouthful of pizza. '*No!* I told you. This guy looks like he just walked off a catwalk.' She shook her head in a decisive movement. 'It's more likely he happily whipped of his shirt because he forgot I was female.'

Her friend narrowed her eyes. 'That's a pile of crap and you know it. You're gorgeous.'

Said with the certainty only a best friend could manage.

'I'm not gorgeous,' Lanie said, and waved her hand dismissively when Teagan went to speak again. 'Not in the way people like Grayson Manning are. Or my sister. My mum, even. I'm just not one of the beautiful people. And, honestly, if it means I'd carry on like Gray does, I really don't mind my ungorgeousness.'

Teagan shook her head in disagreement, but thankfully kept silent.

It had been a great disappointment to Sandra Smith that her eldest daughter had inherited not only the height and athleticism of her ex-husband, but unfortunately also the strong features that were arresting in a man but not exactly beautiful in women. Thankfully two years later Sienna had come along, and was every bit as beauty-pageant-pretty as Sandra.

'So what are his latest efforts?' Teagan asked, picking up the unspoken cue to change the subject. 'Other than the emergency shirt-shopping expedition?'

Lanie shrugged. 'Same old, same old. Letting me know he needs me to write up a report five minutes before five— so I'm there until seven. Or asking me to book the best restaurant in Perth that is fully booked, for a very important lunch meeting—so I have to go down there and sweet-talk a table out of them. And then cancelling said meeting. Plus, of course, just the general expectation that I can read his mind.'

Teagan shook her head. 'You shouldn't put up with this, you know. I'm starting to feel bad. This guy isn't normal—trust me.'

An unwanted flashback to that more-than-a-glimpse of incredible bare chest she'd seen in Gray's office very much underlined that comment. No, Gray was *not* normal. She didn't understand why, but somehow in his office his chest had been just so much more *naked* than at the beach. It had felt personal.

Intimate.

She put her half-eaten pizza slice back down on her plate, suddenly no longer hungry.

'You *can* quit, you know. I'm sure the agency would find you something else—no problem.'

'I know that,' Lanie said. 'But it's not so bad. It pays almost double my salary at the swim centre, and I wouldn't get that anywhere else—anyone but Gray would see straight through my total lack of experience.'

Teagan's eyes narrowed. 'There you go again. Underselling yourself.'

Lanie snorted with her wine glass in mid-air. 'No. You were the one that *oversold* me, remember?'

Teagan rolled her eyes dramatically. 'A small detail. The fact is this guy has an awesome PA and he should know it. He's taking you for granted. Most people would've quit by now.'

Based on what she'd learnt in the Manning lunch room, most had. Lanie had a sneaky suspicion that one of the guys in Legal was running a book on how long she'd last.

'Teags, I could deliver his twice a day triple-shot latte nude and he wouldn't notice.'

Disturbingly, her friend's eyes widened. 'That's *it!*'

'I'm not flashing Gray Manning, Teagan,' she said dryly.

'No, no. Not that—at least not exactly.'

'Partial nudity, then?' Lanie said. 'You know, I reckon if I borrowed one of Sienna's skirts it would be so short and so small that—'

'You're not taking this seriously.'

Lanie raised her eyebrows. 'I didn't realise *you* were.'

Teagan's wine glass made a solid thunk as she placed it firmly on the table. She leant forward, meeting her eyes across the half-finished pizza.

'*Make* him notice you. *Make* him appreciate you.'

'And what would be the point?'

'Because you deserve it.'

It was lovely, really, what Teagan was doing. Lovely, and kind, and all the things that Teagan's friendship always was. Plus also one of the things it occasionally was.

Misguided.

'I'm fine, Teags,' she said. 'Really.'

She didn't need Teagan—or Gray as her proxy—to be her cheerleader.

She knew Teagan was worried about her—worried about how she was handling the continuing publicity around Sienna and her success.

But she was fine. She had a new job that paid well. A fresh start.

Not that working for a grumpy property magnate had ever been a particular dream of hers.

She looked across at Teagan. 'So you can put the pink hair dye or whatever you were planning on hold for now.'

'I was thinking more along the lines of a gorilla suit, but...'

And then they both laughed, and Gray and his shirtlessness was—mostly—forgotten amongst talk of Teagan's latest disaster date, the cooking-related reality TV show they were both hooked on, and anything and everything else.

Except, of course, swimming. Or Sienna.

* * *

Lanie's phone rang far too early the next morning.

She rolled over in the narrow single bed she'd grown up in, reaching out blindly with one hand towards her bedside table. Typically, she managed to knock the phone to the floor rather than grab it, so it took another twenty seconds of obnoxious ringing and fumbling around on her hands and knees in the inky darkness before said phone was located.

'Hello?' she said.

She'd been too disorientated to read the name on the screen, and besides it was most likely Sienna. Her sister hadn't quite managed to figure out the whole time difference thing.

'I need you to come over.'

The voice was deep and male. Definitely not her sister.

Lanie blinked in the semi-darkness. Dawn light was attempting to push its way under the edge of the bedroom's blinds with little effect.

'*Gray?*' she asked, although it was a rhetorical question. Of course it was. 'Do you know what time it is?'

'I have a flight to Singapore that's boarding in a few hours' time—so, yes, I do.'

There was a long moment of silence as Lanie considered hanging up on him.

'Oh,' he said eventually. 'I'm sorry. I woke you.'

Lucky.

'Can you come over?' he repeated. 'Now?'

'I'd rather not,' she said honestly. 'What's the emergency?'

Now it was Gray's turn to go silent. 'Oh…' he said again, and his surprise that she hadn't just dropped everything to come to his aid was apparent even in that single syllable.

At work Lanie could roll her eyes at his unreasonable requests—probably not as subtly as she should—or she could tell herself it was her job or whatever. But just before five in the morning…

No. There was a line, and Gray had definitely just stepped over it.

'It's my dog,' he said.

Instantly Lanie felt terrible. 'Is he okay?'

'Yes,' Gray said. 'But I forgot to organise someone to walk and feed him. Rodney used to sort it out for me, but I guess I didn't mention it to you.'

Lanie supposed he got points for not making *that* somehow her fault.

'And you couldn't e-mail me about it?'

'No,' he said. 'I need you to come over now so I can explain what he eats and where to walk him, and—'

'Okay, okay,' she interrupted on a sigh. There was no point asking him to write it down. Gray just didn't work—or think—like that. In his head it would be far more efficient for her to come over and for him to tell her. 'I'm coming over.'

Ten minutes later she knocked on Gray's front door. He lived only a few kilometres away from her, but unsurprisingly his house was right on the beach. It was gorgeous in an angular, modern, mansion-like way. At this hour of the morning the street was silent, save for the muffled crash of waves.

The door swung open, but before she could even say hello his back was to her as he walked away, already shooting out instructions. Luther, at least, bothered to greet her. He sat obediently for his welcome pats, then pressed his head against her thigh as she followed Gray down the hall. Lanie had thrown on an old tracksuit, and her sandals thwacked loudly against the pale, glossy porcelain tiles.

'So, Luther is a red setter,' Gray was explaining. 'And he's on this special prescribed diet as he has a few allergies. It's *essential* he only eats this food...' Gray opened up one of the many, many drawers in a huge granite and glass kitchen to point at neatly labelled tubs of dog biscuits. 'Otherwise he gets sick and—well, you don't want to know what sort of mess that makes.'

Lanie raised an eyebrow as she considered the size of Luther and the fact that every bit of the house she could see was decorated in shades of white and cream. 'I can imagine.'

Gray met her eyes for a second and one side of his mouth quirked upwards. 'I'd advise you not to.'

Automatically, she grinned back.

When he smiled, his face was transformed. She wouldn't say his expression softened—there was something far too angular and intense about Gray—but there was certainly a lightness, a freshness. And a cheeky, intriguing sparkle to his gaze.

Lanie took a step backwards and promptly walked into a tall stainless steel bin. Some sensor contraption obediently flipped the lid open, and the unexpected movement made Lanie jump and bump her hip—hard—against the benchtop.

'You okay?' Gray asked.

'Other than it being far too early in the morning for me to be co-ordinated?' she replied, raising a pointed eyebrow.

Nicely covered, she thought, giving herself a mental shake. The last thing she needed was another confusing beside-the-taxi or shirt-off moment.

'Sorry about that,' he said, not sounding sorry at all. He'd already walked off again, continuing his monologue.

Lanie rubbed the small, rapidly forming bruise on her hip as Gray described how this section of the house was secured separately from the rest and about some nifty automatic heating and lighting system he'd had installed so that Luther would be comfortable. Plus there was a Luther-sized door to the landscaped pool and garden that Lanie could now just see in the very early rays of sun.

At the end of his explanation, in front of a neat row of hooks hung with multi-coloured leads, Gray finished with a flourish, 'So Luther is *totally* fine whenever I go away.'

But Gray wasn't looking at her, he was looking at Luther, who had stretched himself out, oblivious, at their feet.

'You don't sound all that convinced.'

This whipped Gray's attention back to her. 'Of course I'm—' he started. Then, suddenly he crouched down and rubbed the big dog's head right behind his ears. He looked up to meet Lanie's gaze. 'No, you're right. I hate leaving him behind. Leaving him here is better than boarding him, but not much.' Another pause. 'I'll give you a list of walkers I've used before, and a couple to avoid—'

'I'll look after him,' Lanie said. She'd assumed she would be, anyway. Another invisible line on her job description: *Responsible for the care and walking of Mr Manning's red setter as required.*

'Are you sure?'

Lanie nodded. 'No problem. Although I'd rather take him home to my place, if that's okay? Easier than coming here twice a day.'

Gray smiled, again—a big, genuine smile—and Lanie found herself smiling back almost as hugely. It was impossible to do anything else in the presence of such high-wattage charm.

But then his brow furrowed. 'Do you have any experience with dogs?'

His obvious worry for his pet was beyond endearing. Luther rolled onto his back, baring his pale golden tummy in a silent plea: *scratches, please.*

'I grew up with a collection of my mother's small, fluffy lapdog terrors—honestly, anything Luther throws at me will be child's play. Besides,' she said, dropping to her knees to administer the demanded tummy-rubs and directing her next comment to the dog, 'Luther and I have an understanding— don't we, mate? I am the thrower of the ball—but he owns it.'

She grinned as she darted a glance at Gray.

'That's about right,' he said. 'He'll also love you for ever if you walk him down at North Cottesloe beach. It's his favourite.'

'I know,' Lanie said, slowing her hand's movement down to a glacial pace.

Gray's brow had refurrowed and he looked at her quizzically, as if she'd just said something very odd. 'How do you know?'

Lanie blinked. Her hand had gone completely still, and Luther writhed about on the floor a bit, apparently hoping to somehow wring another pat from her listless touch.

'Because I walk down at North Cottesloe beach. *All the time.*'

'Really?' Gray said. He was so close to her, kneeling by Luther's head.

He bumped his shoulder slightly with hers as he stood, and reached out to steady her. Instantly her skin went all tingly and warm.

'Yes,' she said, quite firmly. 'I walk most mornings. I see you and Luther a lot. You wave.'

At some point Lanie had stood too, and Gray dropped his hand from her upper arm.

'Oh...' Gray said, no longer in concerned-and-rather-adorable-dog-owner mode, but in vague-when-it-comes-to-everything-but-Manning mode. 'To be honest the beach is kind of my time out. I don't really pay attention to much at all.'

No. Definitely no points for that total lack of an apology. She'd convinced herself it was okay that he'd never connected her to that original morning they'd met because he'd noticed her now. He made the effort to wave. It had felt friendly—like a form of camaraderie or something. As if they were a team.

It was that guy on the beach with his dog that she reminded herself of when Gray was being particularly unreasonable, or autocratic, or pushy—or whatever other negative phrase she wanted to use to describe her boss.

But it wasn't even real.

Lanie was silent as Gray handed her a dog lead. He was

saying something about how he'd go and grab Luther's bed, and bowls and food to put in her car.

She watched his retreating back. He was in casual clothing for his flight—a faded old T-shirt, jeans that rode low on his hips. His shoulders were broad, and he had the type of strong, muscled legs that could never wear the currently fashionable, hipster skinny-guy jeans.

He was gorgeous and perfect—the type of guy that you didn't forget.

But the girl he worked with eight hours a day was evidently not worth noticing even when he looked directly at her and waved.

Gray had made her feel invisible that first day at the beach *and* ever since.

And Lanie Smith was *not* going to let that happen again.

CHAPTER FIVE

A MAKEOVER WAS not particularly original, Lanie knew. And Teagan had insisted it wasn't necessary—but she was just being kind.

Lanie did know—in an absent, better-get-round-to-it-at-some-point way—that she needed a haircut. And that the few suits she owned were nearly five years out of fashion and better suited to her at her race weight—not with the extra five odd kilos she was carrying now. *And* that it probably wouldn't hurt to slap on some make-up each morning. There was no chlorine fog to make her eyes water and her mascara run at Manning, after all.

So—a makeover it was.

Lanie twisted to slide the skirt's zip closed, then fussed for a few moments, tucking and plucking at the cream silk blouse.

She smoothed her hands down the fine wool fabric of the skirt, enjoying how it felt against her palms. The price tag dangled just above her hip, and she traced the sharp edges of the thick card with her fingers.

It was silly to delay the inevitable, but she wanted to enjoy how the clothes felt for as long as possible. Right now, before she turned to face the mirror, she could pretend she looked as good in this outfit as the mannequin also wearing it on the shop floor.

She wouldn't say she hated to shop—not exactly. She appreciated beautiful clothing, and was regularly tempted to try on the clothes displayed in shop windows—although she rarely did.

Like Gray, she had a tendency to shop in bulk—but unlike Gray she didn't do it in the name of efficiency. It was more that clothes and Lanie just didn't get along.

The way she imagined she'd look when she first saw the dress, or top or jacket on the rack and the way she *actually* looked never quite matched.

But this part she liked. Before she turned to face the mirror. The possibility that *this* outfit might look as amazing as she'd hoped.

'Come *on*, Lanie!' Teagan knocked on the change-room door impatiently. 'How does it look?'

Lanie shook her head as if to clear her thoughts. She was being ridiculous. Melodramatic. 'Just a sec.'

She spun around.

She looked…not bad.

Intellectually, she knew that.

The slim cut skirt helped emphasise what waist she had, and the delicate embroidery around the V neckline helped draw attention away from her broad shoulders. She stood up on her tiptoes to mimic heels and noted that her legs looked good—long and athletic.

Which, of course, was the thing. No matter the clothes or the shoes she was still tall, still strong and still slightly awkward. That was how people described her: *athletic.* Not elegant, or beautiful. And definitely not willowy—a descriptor regularly associated with Sienna.

But I'm lucky to be so tall, to have such strong shoulders. It's why I swim so fast...

She flung the door open, striking a pose. 'What do you think?'

Teagan clapped her hands together. 'Fabulous!'

It took a huge effort not to raise a sceptical eyebrow, but she managed. Teagan would only argue with her, anyway.

Her friend had a small mountain of clothes in her arms and she shoved them in Lanie's direction. 'Here—try these.'

'You know,' Teagan said through the door when Lanie was back in the change-room, 'it seems a shame to waste all these outfits just on Grayson Manning.'

'They're not really *for* Gray,' Lanie said carefully. She absently assessed the charcoal-coloured shift dress she wore—not good: it made what shape she had disappear entirely—before meeting her own gaze in the mirror. This and her upcoming visit to a hairdresser and beautician wasn't about looking good for Gray. It was about her not feeling invisible any more.

Teagan made a dismissive noise. 'Whatever. You look hot. You should come out with me one night.'

'I don't know—'

'And you can't use the early-morning training excuse any more.'

'It wasn't an *excuse*,' Lanie corrected gently. 'It was a fact. I was training to make the Australian team—not the local swimming carnival.'

'But you're not training now,' Teagan said—not unkindly, but with some emphasis. 'And you definitely need to start dating men who aren't *swimmers*.'

Lanie grinned at Teagan's tone as she tugged the dress off over her head. 'You make it sound like they have gills or something.'

'It's all that waxing they do,' Teagan said, and Lanie could just imagine her friend's look of distaste. 'It's not natural.'

Lanie laughed out loud. 'Fair point.'

She grabbed the next piece of clothing from the hook—another dress, this one in shades of chocolate, with a peplum detail at the waist.

'Although,' Teagan continued, 'I reckon I'd be happy if you dated *anyone*. It's been far too long. It can't be good for you.'

Lanie laughed again, but it was a touch more forced.

'What? A date a month keeps the doctor away or something?'

She stepped into the dress and tugged it upwards a little roughly.

Teagan snorted. 'Honey—a *month?* That would be awesome. But I reckon we're talking a year since that guy...what was his name?'

'Dominic. And it's not been a year.'

Although as she contorted herself inelegantly in front of the mirror to do up the back zip, Lanie did the calculations. Teagan was right—it *had* been a year. Fourteen months, actually.

And it had hardly been some amazing love affair. A guy she'd met at the swim centre. A good handful of dates over a month or so. He'd stayed over a night or two—but then she'd ended it.

She'd wanted to focus on her swimming—in fact she'd *needed* to. She'd known how hard she'd have to work to make the team and she hadn't been able to afford any distractions. Especially the distraction of a relationship in which she felt they were simply going through the motions.

Swimming had come first. *Always.*

Dress finally on, she pushed open the door to show Teagan.

'Oh, this is *definitely* my favourite!' her friend gushed.

Lanie turned this way and that in front of the mirrors that lined the wall across from the change room. She still looked like a tall, slightly gawky Amazon—but the dress worked her curves for all they were worth. 'It's nice...'

Teagan rolled her eyes. 'You're a lost cause, Lanie-girl,' she said. Stepping forward, she reached out to grab her hand. 'But I meant it before—you need to get out more. You've worked so hard for so long, you deserve to have some fun.'

'Mmm-hmm,' she said, and ignored Teagan's raised eyebrow. 'But for now I'm focussing on exorcising Ms Invisible, okay?'

* * *

Gray kept staring at their hands.

One was young, pale and perfect. Tipped with subtle pink polish, the fingers were laced through her husband's much larger, much *older* fingers. His nails were cut short and straight across in a neat contrast to the skin of his hands, which looked slightly oversized and baggy, scattered with the occasional sunspot—gained golfing, Gray could only presume, as his father hadn't exactly spent his working days outside.

Their hands lay linked on the crisp white tablecloth, between the fine china and sparkling cutlery of the table settings.

Tasha laughed musically at something Gordon had said, staring up at him with adoration. Gordon smiled back—a familiar smile. Loving and equally adoring.

Gray had seen it all before.

He looked back at their hands. Somehow it was *their hands* that surprised him.

He shouldn't be surprised. Tasha was wife number seven. Yes, *seven*.

He'd been here before—to dinners just like this one, organised by the eager new wife, keen to establish a relationship between herself and her new 'son'. Not that any in the past twenty years had been stupid enough to refer to him in that way.

He knew this dinner—knew the infatuated smiles, knew he'd drive home tonight and wonder where exactly his father would buy this latest wife's new home when they inevitably divorced. He might even wonder whether his dad ever worried that his ex-wives would bump into each other at the local, ritzy, over-priced organic grocery store.

Gray knew the answer to that: *no*. His father had perfected the art of the amicable divorce. A multi-million-dollar home as a parting gift possibly expedited that goal.

Yet tonight he was surprised.

Because tonight his dad looked old.

Not just older-than-his-new-wife old—he'd been that for the past three wives, quite spectacularly—but just plain old, *old.*

He looked like a man with a thirty-five-year-old son who'd had said son when pushing forty himself. He looked retired. He looked like a smartly dressed, smartly groomed *old* guy.

Gray's eyes were drawn back to their hands again. Tasha was rubbing her thumb back and forth along his dad's knuckles.

It should have looked loving and sweet. Maybe it did.

To Gray, it looked obscene.

With a glance and a nod in Tasha's direction he excused himself from the table. He wouldn't leave—he'd done that once before, years ago, and the wife of that moment had been devastated. It had *not* been worth the subsequent months of that wife trying far too hard—and his father being angry with him.

He couldn't even remember why he'd walked out that time. This time he just needed space, some fresh air. His dad's place was a penthouse at the opposite end of the terrace to the Manning offices. The balcony was huge, but mostly empty, with moonlight reflecting off the panes of the bifold doors and something sparkly mixed into the pavers.

Gray walked to the railing, wrapping his fingers around the smooth, cool metal, and stared out, unseeing, to the spectacular Swan River. On the other side of the water streetlights edged the South Perth foreshore, and to his right headlights glowed as they crossed the Narrows Bridge in a steady stream.

'What was that about?'

His father's voice was gruff, but not angry, behind him.

Gray turned slowly and shrugged. 'I'm tired.'

He'd flown in from Singapore only hours before. His meetings hadn't gone as well as he'd expected. He'd hoped he'd be flying home with a signed contract. He wasn't.

Was he different without the reassurance of his father in the background? He didn't really believe that. He'd never needed his dad to hold his hand.

Next week he'd fly out again, this time to Vietnam: a new resort on China Beach and a tour for potential investors of the villas already built. He was determined to be on his game. To be the Grayson Manning he'd been the rest of his career.

'What do you think?' his dad asked.

It took Gray a moment or two to work out what his dad meant.

Oh, Tasha. He shrugged again. 'She seems nice.'

He'd never met her before. His dad didn't have elaborate weddings any more—he did Las Vegas, or Bali or—as this time—Fiji. He didn't even bother telling his son about it.

Not that Gray telling his dad what he *really* thought would have made any difference.

Why are you doing it, Dad? What's the point?

He knew the answer to that question, too: *Why not? I love her.*

Right.

And that theory had worked so well the previous six times.

For a brilliant businessman, renowned for his hard bargaining and measured decisions, Gordon Manning's approach to his love-life made absolutely no sense.

It went against everything Gray had been taught. He modelled his business manner on his father's—the way he never let emotion cloud his decisions. The way he always took the time to fully understand or analyse everything. His steely, unflappable nature in the boardroom. And yet Gordon had retired and walked out of that boardroom and—it would seem—straight into the arms of sales assistant Tasha. Three months later they were married.

Gray shouldn't be surprised.

But he was disappointed.

This obsession with the idea of love—and not just any love, but insta-love—and his bizarrely unwavering faith in the idea of marriage despite all evidence to the contrary, was his dad's quirk.

Quirk? Weakness would be more accurate.

'Tell me about Singapore,' his dad said.

Gray propped his weight against the balcony railing. Even in the limited light out here it was clear that his father was in default mode. The sharp, shrewd, intelligent mode that Gray was familiar with. The one that he understood, admired and respected.

Not sooky, moony, head-in-the-clouds mode, while his much younger wife caressed his weathered skin.

That version of his father embarrassed him.

'Singapore was fine,' Gray said.

He wasn't going to elaborate. He didn't even consider it. He'd had almost twenty years of grooming from his dad and he'd just been confirming Gray's instincts for much of the past decade. Whatever his clients and investors might think, he *didn't* need his father's advice.

Gordon raised an eyebrow. For the first time Gray noticed that it was made up of more grey than raven-black.

'You're retired, Dad. You've got more important things to worry about,' he said. He even nodded meaningfully towards the kitchen, where he could see the slim figure of Tasha as she fussed about busily.

It wasn't sincere and Gordon knew it.

But still his father didn't push. Instead he reached out and gripped Gray's upper arm. Gray was wearing a T-shirt and jeans—straight off the plane—and his dad's touch was surprisingly firm and warm where it overlapped cotton and skin.

He met Gray's eyes. They were a near mirror image of his own, the colour an exact reflection. His expression was intense and knowing.

But he wouldn't push. He never had. He'd once said Gray did enough pushing on his own.

'You're right there, son,' he said with false heartiness. 'But I've got to tell you, Gray, you're missing out. About time you settled down.'

Gray pasted on a false smile, managing a laugh, even. 'Maybe one day, Dad.'

But Gordon knew that was false and insincere too.

Because Gray had worked too hard to risk all that he'd achieved on something as fleeting, as distracting and as superfluous as *love*.

His father's relationships—and his own—were yet to convince him of anything different. At least he had the good sense to end his affairs after a few weeks or months, rather than taking his father's rather extreme option and getting married.

Together, Gray and Gordon walked back inside, their joint re-entrance eliciting a mega-watt grin from Tasha. This was familiar too—the new wife's concern that she had somehow formed a wedge between father and son.

Gray should tell her she had nothing to worry about.

Gordon and Gray's relationship never changed. And so it would remain—long after Tasha, in a shower of expensive parting gifts, was gone.

'Now, don't you look lovely!'

Bob grinned down at her, order notebook in hand. Lanie leant back in her chair to smile back up at him. Beside her Luther sat obediently, his liquid brown eyes beautifully pleading in Bob's direction.

'Thanks.' She reached up to tuck a strand of newly highlighted hair behind her ear. 'Just the usual,' she said. Bob didn't take the hint.

'Guess you didn't swim today if your hair's still looking fancy?'

Lanie forced her smile to remain in place. 'Nope,' she said firmly. 'Haven't swum in months. And you know what? I don't miss it at all.'

Bob's mouth formed into a perfectly horizontal line. He took a deep breath, as if he was going to speak again—but then didn't. Instead he slowly—he wasn't young, after all—dropped down to a squat in front of Gray's dog. As he'd done on each of the four days that Gray had been away, Bob miraculously produced a small bone treat—which Luther took, very politely.

The speed which he ate it was less so.

Bob headed back to his shiny chrome coffee machine without another word, and Lanie shifted in her seat so she could stare back out across the street to the ocean.

She could make a good guess at what Bob had been about to say. That he believed she should still be swimming was obvious. It was bizarre. Everybody else—the selectors, her coach, her team mates…heck, *herself*…had known it was the right time for her to retire. She wasn't going to be making some great comeback. She was done.

Everyone knew that—except for the kind old man who worked at her local café.

It was sweet, she supposed. Well intended. She was sure he didn't mean to make her feel uncomfortable whenever he asked his daily question.

And, to be honest, she didn't have a clue why she *did* feel uncomfortable. If anyone asked her if she'd made the right decision she'd answer immediately and honestly: *Yes, I have.*

So, yeah—it was a bit weird…that he asked her and that she reacted as she did.

It was getting warmer now—not summer-warm, but warm enough that in the sun like this, summer didn't feel quite so far away.

More people were at the beach each morning, too. Not Gray. He'd flown back from Singapore yesterday and then gone straight to a dinner. He'd wanted to come and collect Luther afterwards, but Lanie had been clear that it really was no trouble having him another night.

Besides, she hadn't really wanted Gray turning up at her house late at night. Her flannelette pyjamas did *not* feed into her plan.

Flannelette pyjamas were Ms Invisible.

Next time she saw Gray she was determined he'd be paying attention.

Also—she really didn't want to give Luther up just yet. Lanie reached out to rub him behind his ears and the big dog leant immediately—blissfully—against her.

She'd loved looking after Luther. Loved having a silent companion on her daily beach walks and the way he lay on her kitchen floor as she cooked.

She'd never considered a pet before—between her rigorous training schedule, her full-time job, regular travel for swim meets and the tiny apartment she lived in, it just hadn't been possible.

Lanie's lips quirked upwards. Except for the size of her place, they were exactly the same reasons she'd remained mostly single her entire adult life.

But she guessed things were different now.

Everything was.

Gray was already in his office—door closed—when Lanie arrived at work an hour and a half later.

She felt good. So far Caroline at Reception had complimented her on her new suit, while Marilyn had said lots of nice things about her hair—wanting to know the name of her salon, no less.

Not that she'd gone crazy with her efforts today. Some women looked like different people when they were made up—but Lanie wasn't one of them. She'd been genetically blessed with a few good things—long, thickish eyelashes, for one, and clear, smooth skin, for another. A bit wasted on her average-coloured eyes and too strong features, she felt—but hey, she wasn't complaining.

But even though she was wearing mascara and foundation today—and even a bit of eyeliner—Lanie didn't feel she looked all that stunningly different.

The clothes she'd bought with Teagan were probably the bigger statement. Well-fitting, and a size larger, her new pencil skirt and pretty salmon-coloured blouse flattered her shape rather than pulling against it. And combined with her hair—now cut in layers and with generous splashes of blond—it *was* quite an improvement.

So, while she hadn't exactly turned up as a different person—she didn't aspire too, anyway—she *did* look good.

Lanie was putting the finishing touches on a report—some impressive statistics related to the success of Manning's Singapore residential developments over the past five years—when the little instant messenger bar at the bottom of her desktop screen started to flash impatiently.

She clicked on it and a window popped up.

IMON

This was Gray's very own acronym: *In My Office Now.*

No *please*, of course. As usual, her jaw clenched and she silently seethed.

She'd come up with a series of her own acronyms, and her fingers itched to type them as they hovered just about the keyboard: *WPF—When Pigs Fly.* Or… *SYASNN—Since You Asked So Nicely, No.*

But instead she stood, straightened her shoulders, and brushed her hands down the fabric of her blouse and skirt. For now, this job was serving a purpose. So she held her tongue/fingers.

She grabbed a notepad and walked in her shiny, trendy new heels into Gray's office.

As usual, he didn't look up when she walked in. He was focussed entirely on his computer screen and instead simply waved vaguely in the direction of one of the chairs across from his desk.

This was part of the routine. The alternative was that he'd just start talking—or rather, barking directions. The fact he'd waved at the chair simply meant this was going to be longer than a ten-second conversation.

Lanie smiled. *Conversation.* Right.

Her tummy felt unexpectedly light and butterflyish as she walked to the chair.

Nerves.

She did her best to ignore them.

She settled into the chair, notebook at the ready. 'How can I help?'

Now Gray looked up. A quick glance—lightning-quick. He barely met her gaze before his attention returned to his computer.

'Have you booked my flights to Hoi An for next week?'

'Last week,' she said. 'You're flying direct to Ho Chi Minh, then a second flight to Da Nang. A car will meet you at the airport.'

She waited impatiently for him to look up. To notice the changes—to, for once, properly look at her.

He nodded, still staring at the screen. 'Do you have a passport?'

Lanie blinked. 'Yes.'

She'd renewed it leading up to the championships, so it was perfect and stamp-free.

'Right. I want you to come with me. Can you sort that out?'

'You want me to come to Vietnam?'

Finally he glanced up, as if surprised by her question. 'Isn't that what I just said?'

This time he did pause for a second, to catch her gaze.

Then his attention flicked over her—her hair, her face, maybe her clothes. Very brief.

Had he noticed?

Anything?

He typed something on his keyboard, the subtle click of each key seeming particularly loud today.

She knew what this was: she'd been dismissed.

She was supposed to go away and book her flights and that was that. Gray's brain had already ticked over to his next task.

He probably wasn't even entirely aware that she hadn't left the room.

'Why?' she asked.

Gray's head jerked up. As expected, his expression was very much: *Why are you still here?*

'Because I want you there.'

Again back to his screen and his oh-so-important e-mail.

'What if I have plans?' Lanie asked. 'The trip is over a weekend. I could have somewhere terribly important to be.'

Gray pushed back his chair a little and leant back. His gaze shifted a little. Focussed.

'Do you?'

Lanie shrugged. 'That isn't the point. If you can explain to me the reason why I need to jet off across the world at a moment's notice, I can then weigh up whether or not I'm able to do it.'

'Vietnam is hardly across the—'

'That isn't the point either,' she said.

Did his lips quirk up just momentarily? Lanie couldn't be sure.

'I thought everyone wanted to go to Vietnam. It's very beautiful.'

Lanie shrugged. 'I'd love to go to Vietnam—' she started, and immediately saw Gray's eyes unfocus. He thought it was sorted. The issue filed away. 'On a holiday. *Not* with my boss.'

The glint returned to his gaze. Another blink-and-you'd-miss it sense of a smile flicked across his lips.

'Right,' he said. He crossed his arms, but his attention remained on her. He cleared his throat. 'I'd like you to accompany me as this project is particularly important to Manning. We require further investors for a new luxury beachfront hotel. Interest hasn't been as I'd hoped, so the purpose of this trip is quite simply to convince a group of wavering investors that there is nothing better they could do with their money than hand it over to us for this project. I'll be there for three days—wining, dining, etcetera, etcetera.' His lack of enthusiasm for this task was obvious. 'I need you to keep me organised, to deal with the details I tend to forget. You did a great job while I was in Singapore, but our being in different countries is not ideal. It would be much more efficient to have you there with me.'

That was about the most Gray had ever said to her at once. He tended to talk in soundbites, and very much on a need-to-know basis.

Something else occurred to her. 'I assume I'll be paid overtime?'

He nodded. 'Of course.'

Lanie narrowed her eyes as she looked at Gray, as if she was carefully considering his request.

He held her gaze the entire time.

'Okay,' she said, after what she figured was enough time for him to stew about it. 'I'll come.'

Gray nodded sharply, then stood—and surprised her by holding out his hand.

She stared at it for a moment, before making herself step forward and reaching out her own hand to grip his.

His touch was firm and warm. Lanie felt a blush start to build somewhere around her chest and begin to creep upwards. No slower than the day when he'd stripped off his shirt and definitely no less heated.

And a blush just wouldn't do. Not now. She made sure her gaze remained firmly trained on his. Clear and direct, not flustered.

'Thank you,' Gray said.

Lanie dropped her hand from his as soon as she could. Immediately it was easier to think, and for the cogs to start moving again in her brain.

'Not a problem,' she said, although her voice cracked a little and she needed to clear her throat. 'I'll get back to work, then. I'll need to sort out my visa immediately.'

But now she was speaking to the top of his head. He'd sat back down.

'Mmm-hmm,' he said, reverting to the Gray she was familiar with.

Although that was okay. Because today she certainly hadn't been invisible—and it had *nothing* to do with her new hair or new clothes.

But what had she hoped to achieve, really? Did she want Gray to think she was attractive?

No. He was her boss.

Liar.

It was like that first morning at the beach. She wouldn't be human if she hadn't noticed Gray Manning running along the shore with the sun glistening off his sweat-sheened biceps. And wondered…

She wouldn't be human if she didn't want to impress a man like Gray.

And today he had noticed her—when for the first time in a very long time she'd said exactly what she was thinking. She hadn't censored herself—not for Gray, and not for herself.

Not the way she did when she told people she was okay after missing out on team selection. *'I swam a personal best. I did everything I could. I'm proud of getting this far. Of course I'm okay.'*

Not like telling Sienna how happy she was for her, telling her not to waste any time worrying about her. *'This is your moment, Sienna! I'm so proud of you, and that's all that matters.'*

And not like telling Teagan that she was fine working in a job that was so far removed from her dreams and aspirations that it was laughable—and that she was frankly terrified that she had nothing new on the horizon. Nothing new to strive for. *'It's actually really great, Teags, to have this time to recalibrate. To think. I feel really relaxed, really calm—don't worry about me!'*

Today she'd spoken her mind—over something trivial, but still—and it had felt *great*. Better than the way she'd felt when Caroline had admired her suit or Marilyn had been sweet about her hair.

It was a tiny thing. A baby step.

But she knew she was going to do it again.

CHAPTER SIX

THE HUMIDITY, THICK and cloying, enveloped Lanie as she stepped from the plane onto the mobile staircase that led to the Tarmac. She'd worn jeans for the flight—perfect for Perth in August, but not ideal for Vietnam at the very beginning of the wet season. She could feel the heavy fabric clinging to her with every step as she headed for the bus that would whisk them the short distance to the terminal.

'Don't worry, we're about two minutes away from air-conditioning,' Gray said beside her, rolling up the sleeves of his shirt as he walked.

Lanie nodded, glancing in his direction. She'd half expected him to be completely unaffected by the weather—one of those perfect people who were always effortlessly cool and stylish, as if in their own separate temperature-controlled micro-climate.

Although she supposed she was already quite aware that he did, in fact, sweat. A disturbingly photographic memory of Gray running shirtless along the white sand of North Cottesloe beach flashed unhelpfully across Lanie's brain. She gave her head a little shake and cleared her throat.

Focus.

The small bus was almost full of tourists. Backpacker-types with nut-brown tans, families from toddlers up to grandparents, and a few couples that Lanie would put good money on being honeymooners, with their arms intertwined and bodies touching, despite the oppressive heat.

It was a different crowd from the arrivals in Ho Chi Minh a few hours earlier. There the plane had also had its fair share of travellers in business attire—quite fitting for Vietnam's bustling, rapidly developing economic centre and its population of more than twenty million. All Lanie had seen was the airport while in transit, but even so the sense of sheer activity had been apparent, and she wished she'd had the opportunity to venture outside and witness the uniquely crazy street traffic for which Vietnam was famous.

But Da Nang airport served a tourist centre and here life already felt slower. Although when she walked into the terminal Lanie quickly realised that *slower* was relative.

She'd expected something smaller. She'd been told by friends of a single baggage carousel and walls plastered with posters for local hotels and the tailors that Hoi An was famous for. Instead she was greeted by what seemed like acres of shiny tiles and high raked ceilings. Very modern, very international—not at all the regional Vietnam she'd expected.

'The new terminal opened about a year ago,' Gray explained as they waited to collect their bags. 'You could say that this area has well and truly been discovered by tourists. It's no longer a closely guarded secret.'

'That's why we're here,' Lanie said.

'Exactly.'

And although it was silly—after all, she didn't know any different—she felt a little disappointed that she hadn't been here earlier—before tourism and investors just like Manning had swooped.

Once they had their bags they headed outside into another wall of heat, and a crowd of neatly dressed men touting their taxi services. Many came right up close, offering to take their bags, wanting to know where they were staying, and insisting they could offer *'a very good price.'*

Everyone was smiling, and no one touched her—and yet it wasn't what Lanie had expected. She found herself shifting nearer to Gray as they walked—close enough to bump into him.

'Oh!' she said, stepping away. 'Sorry.'

But a moment later she bumped into him again, just as Gray told yet another extremely keen driver that they already had a car organized. This time as she went to apologise she felt Gray's hand on the small of her back.

Not wrapped around her. Not pushing her or directing her. Just *there*.

In the heat his touch was—of course—warm. Very warm. It went right through her thin T-shirt to her skin, and his hand felt strong and reassuring.

She let out a breath she'd had no idea she was holding,

His hand didn't move until they arrived at their car—which was low and white and expensive-looking.

A man in a crisp shirt—who *did* look completely unbothered by the weather—opened the rear door for her just as Gray's hand fell away.

'Thank you,' she murmured.

He just smiled and shrugged in response. *Not a problem.*

Gray walked around to the opposite side of the car as Lanie slid onto the creamy leather back seat.

When Gray joined her, the driver—who introduced himself as Quan—presented them both with small, chilled white towels and bottles of icy cold water. The car slid away from the airport almost silently as Lanie and Gray took advantage of both.

'So, what do you think so far?' Gray asked.

Lanie twisted the cap onto her water bottle and placed it back in its little tray between the front seats.

'Overwhelming,' she said, then grinned. 'Although it is kind of silly to be, I guess. I'm taller than *all* the drivers.'

This had only occurred to Lanie as she'd stood directly beside Quan—who was clearly inches shorter than her.

Gray tilted his head as he looked at her. 'Why would that make any difference?' he said. 'It's overwhelming for everyone the first time they come here—me included. I'm a lot taller than you and, trust me, I almost turned around and went back into the terminal the first time I visited.'

The image was so unexpected—tall, strong Grayson Manning hightailing it back into the glossy new terminal—that Lanie laughed out loud. 'Right. Besides, you aren't *that* much taller than me.'

Gray shifted in his seat to face her. 'What are you? Five-eleven?'

She nodded, surprised he'd noticed. 'Exactly.'

'So I've got three inches on you. I win.'

There was a mischievous hint to his tone that was new, and Lanie couldn't help but laugh again. Normally her height triggered comments like *Wow, that's really tall!*—and not in a good way. During her swimming career her body had been her tool, and the breadth of her shoulders and lankiness of her limbs a positive. She'd made herself look at her body objectively and monitored her weight, her skin folds and her lung capacity as if she were a racing car engine.

Yes, she had moments where she envied her more petite sister—when she went clothes-shopping, for instance. Sienna was more reasonably tall, at five foot eight, but with long, narrow feet like flippers and a freakishly good technique. Sienna had an elegance and a *normality* to her—no one ever made jokes about the air being thinner up there, or guessed that she must play basketball or something.

But overall she'd always seen her height as a good thing, and had told herself—firmly—that her moments of self-consciousness were a total waste of time.

More recently she was finding that more difficult. Now she was tall, quite frankly *not* a small person, and she wasn't even an athlete any more. Her size didn't make her special, and it didn't make her a potential champion. It just made her different.

And Gray didn't seem to think it was all that unusual. At all.

Lanie, for the first time since she'd arrived, felt the tension ease from her body. She settled back into her seat, and watched Da Nang city fly past her.

Growing up in Perth, she'd travelled to nearby Bali before, and to Singapore—and her swimming had taken her to Rome a few years ago, and to China. But as the car whisked them through the city the architecture was like nothing she'd ever seen before.

In pretty pastel shades the buildings were sandwiched together—the fronts tall and narrow but their structure stretching out long behind. Above them, power lines criss-crossed each intersection, looking rather alarmingly messily arranged and remarkably copious—as if every home's appliance had its own personal power supply.

Around them, the traffic mingled indiscriminately—luxury cars amongst rusted old overloaded vans—and everywhere, motorbikes. No one, including their own driver, appeared to pay too much attention to the road's lanes, or to progressing in single file. At each stop sign multiple scooters would surround their car and then shoot off ahead, two or three abreast.

And then, just occasionally, Lanie spotted a glimpse of the Vietnam she hadn't even realised she'd been searching for: a man walking along the footpath balancing two baskets from a pole across his shoulders, a woman on a pushbike in simple clothes of beige and brown, her face shaded by a traditional conical hat.

'Oh, did you see her?' she said enthusiastically, when she first saw the woman on her bike, and Gray leant across to see where she was looking. Soon she was asking him questions as Gray pointed out some of the French influences scattered throughout Da Nang—from the red-roofed architecture to the baguettes for sale at cafés alongside traditional Vietnamese *pho* soup.

Soon they'd left Da Nang and joined a busy road towards Hoi An. To their left was the ocean—China Beach—and to the right the marble mountains. More like hills than mountains, they thrust out abruptly from a flat landscape, covered in greenery and dotted with colourful pagodas visible even as the car zoomed past.

The traffic had thinned—not that that stopped the driver of every car or motorbike that came anywhere near them from leaning heavily on his horn. It seemed in Vietnam the horn was more about *Here I am!* rather than *Watch out!*

But soon their car was escaping the noise and the glare of the sun as it turned from the main road down a grand cobblestoned driveway, lushly shaded with towering palms.

Moments later the car came to a stop before a sprawling double-storey building—and here the French influences that Gray had mentioned were immediately apparent. Painted in shades of cream, the red-roofed building boasted elaborately moulded columns and a balcony that stretched across the entire second floor.

The hotel reception area was open-sided, with oversized wicker fans spinning languidly overhead. They were greeted by two women in traditional attire and handed seriously exotic-looking juice concoctions, and watched as their bags were unloaded and silently whisked away.

Gray's phone rang almost immediately. He answered it, making vague hand gestures as he disappeared outside that Lanie could only guess meant he'd be a while. She already knew she had the rest of the afternoon free, so she checked in and then followed another crisply shirted hotel employee to her villa.

It was one thing for Lanie to be familiar with this development through her work with Gray back in Perth—on paper, multi-million-dollar pricetags for a luxury beachside villa weren't all that meaningful—but here, surrounded by this opulent reality, it was something else altogether.

From Reception they passed the main pool area—a series of infinity pools built on different levels, each with uninterrupted views to the private beach. No one swam today, or lay in the canopied daybeds. The hotel was not yet open for business, and none of the private residences had been sold.

Beyond the pools was the beachfront, and here Lanie was deposited at one of the smallest villas—after all, she had no need for multiple bedrooms. Entry was through a private courtyard, lush with thick grass and edged with palms. Inside, the open-plan space was dominated by a raised central section topped with an extravagant four-poster bed. Bifold doors opened out from a small, exquisitely decorated living area to a private deck and then to perfect white sand and the ocean beyond.

It was absolutely beautiful.

Although it had only been a short walk from Reception to her villa, the car's air-conditioning felt like a forgotten memory. Lanie's skin felt over-warm again, despite the cool sanctuary of the villa. There was an obvious solution to that, so she unzipped her suitcase and pulled out a bikini.

With the two pieces of fabric in her hands, she paused.

The swimsuit was new, purchased with Teagan on their shopping trip. The violet-coloured fabric was gorgeous, and it flattered her now slightly less than super-fit shape. It was the perfect bikini to wear at a place like this, but when Lanie thought of the perfect, untouched, unused pools she'd just walked by it didn't feel right at all.

Not the bikini's fault—but she didn't want to laze by a pool, she realised. She didn't even want to simply splash around in the shallows or order a cocktail while she relaxed in crystal-clear water.

She wanted to *swim*. For the first time in ages. And a bikini simply wasn't going to cut it.

Minutes later she'd changed into the plain black one-piece suit she'd packed almost automatically. It was one of her training suits—built for efficiency, not glamour. But it wasn't about to worry her with the possibility of parting from her body at an unfortunate moment, so it was definitely the right suit for today.

She grabbed a fluffy white towel and hit the beach. To her right she could see activity in the distance, but here, on the resort's own beach, there was not another soul. Even the lifeguard's tall white chair was empty. She dumped the towel but resisted the temptation to hit the water immediately—instead she stretched, as she had every morning prior to training for as long as she could remember.

But then—finally—she was in the water. It was warmer than she'd expected, and shallower, so she ducked beneath the water and put further distance between herself and the shore with strong, easy underwater breaststrokes.

Breaking the surface, she treaded water momentarily, looking back towards the shore and the perfect white sand to her beautiful villa.

Lanie grinned. This was surreal—this was *not* where she was supposed to be right now. She and Sienna had had plans to travel together through Europe after the championships—but now it was just Sienna doing the travelling.

And here she was—in Vietnam for *work*, no less.

She was not supposed to be here, but she was unexpectedly glad she was.

Then, with one last look, she turned in the water and with a sure stroke and a powerful kick began to swim.

Gray swiped the phone to end the call, then placed it not entirely gently on the small writing desk in his villa.

Then he swore.

An investor who'd been booked in for the weekend had cancelled.

It should be okay—after all, the personalised tour of the residential properties that Gray had planned for this weekend involved a group of investors. Losing one was no disaster. He knew that, and yet it still bothered him.

Not that the guy had cancelled—it didn't even matter why—but because it had rattled Gray.

On the flight over he'd busied himself on his laptop while running through in his mind exactly how this weekend was going to proceed. In itself, that was not unusual. What *had* been unusual was his demeanour—he'd been tense and fidgety. Fidgety enough to be irrationally annoyed at how Lanie had so obliviously read a paperback for the entire flight, as if she had no idea how much was riding on this trip...

Which, of course, she didn't. And she'd offered numerous times to help during the flight. He'd assured her that she couldn't.

The fact was he'd had nothing to do on the flight either. Everything was sorted. Everything was planned to the nth degree. It *would* go off without a hitch.

There was absolutely no reason why it wouldn't.

He realised he was pacing the floor of his villa from one side of the room to the other, his gaze directed blankly to the limestone tiles.

This was a waste of time.

He needed to go for a run.

Gray's chest heaved as he slowed to a walk. He leant forward, his hands just above his knees, as he took in great, big gulping lungfuls of air.

His body was coated in sweat thanks to the still intense humidity even now, as the sun was just beginning to consider setting. The solution to that problem was obvious, and he'd turned to step towards the welcome waves…when he noticed her.

A long way out a woman was swimming. Her arms moved in confident, practised freestyle movements, her feet kicking up a neat stream of bubbles.

It must be Lanie, he realised—it could be no one else.

He watched her for a few long moments, surprised. Maybe he shouldn't be. She had such a tall and athletic frame it really shouldn't be unexpected that she swam—and swam well.

Not for the first time since that morning after he'd arrived back from Singapore he wondered about her. What did he know about Lanie? She'd shocked him that day with her forthrightness. No one had ever questioned him at work before—at least, not so blatantly. He realised it didn't reflect well upon him—and Marilyn's damn words again came to mind—but, honestly, people didn't say *no* to him. Ever.

But Lanie had. And that intrigued him.

She'd worked for him for weeks. And she'd always been obliging.

Although maybe she hadn't always been. He had a sudden flash of memory of just slightly narrowed eyes, a glint to her gaze. Subtle, but there.

Yes, she'd been obliging. But maybe she hadn't always been happy about it. Or with him.

Actually, that was disingenuous. He *knew* she'd been unimpressed with him at times—the days when he was particularly busy or distracted—and he *knew*—normally some time later—that he'd been less than polite.

But he hadn't really cared.

He'd figured she was being paid to do a job and that was that.

But now…now he was wondering what she really thought.

And as he watched her swim he wondered who she really was.

She'd told him that morning in his house that they'd shared

the beach many a time. He hadn't realised. Even now, considering it, he couldn't remember seeing her. But then, even if pressed, he probably couldn't describe *anyone* he saw at the beach each day. When he ran, he used the time to think. And the times when he couldn't face thinking he'd focus on his breathing. Or the thud of his feet on the sand.

It was just him and Luther and his thoughts—or lack thereof.

It wasn't personal that he'd not noticed her, which is why when he'd seen her reaction that morning—her shock and, hurt—he'd dismissed it.

Gray straightened and ran a hand through his damp hair. Lanie was pretty quick, he'd give her that—she cut through the water effortlessly.

As he watched her he wondered *how* he couldn't have noticed her.

Yes, he'd been focussed on the business. *Entirely* focussed on the business—it was all he did and all he thought about. Except for running.

He prided himself on his focus. Honed it, in fact.

But Lanie somehow—at least momentarily—had him questioning it.

He was intrigued.

In a single movement he pulled off his soaked T-shirt, dumping it on the sand, and—given he ran barefoot—he was instantly ready to swim. He didn't mess around with wading into the water. He simply dived into the shallows, the cool water a welcome relief to his heated skin.

Then he surfaced, spotted Lanie, and began swimming in her direction.

CHAPTER SEVEN

HER STROKES WERE easy. Relaxed.

She wasn't training today. She certainly wasn't racing.

She was just swimming.

Stroke, stroke, stroke, *breathe*. Stroke, stroke, stroke, *breathe*.

Slow. Easy. Effortless.

She wasn't wearing goggles so she kept her eyes shut in the water—besides, there was no blue line for her to watch at the bottom of the ocean.

Every now and again she'd remember to look up between strokes, to check where she was going. But really—aside from the risk of accidentally swimming too far—she was safe. She wasn't about to swim into a stray surfer or a boat.

It was just Lanie and this perfect, gorgeous slice of the South China Sea.

She let her mind wander to anything and everything.

Some of it was silly. She found herself wishing that Bob's little café would miraculously appear on the beach, just so when he asked *'Did you swim today?'* she could declare *Yes!*

But at other times her thoughts turned more serious corners.

Within the reassuring, regular rhythm of her breathing she let herself consider stuff that was far from controlled. Stuff she hadn't let herself consider in weeks. Mainly, *What was she going to do?*

Because—nice and unexpected as this trip to Vietnam was—a career as a personal assistant was not her dream.

She'd spent her life for as long as she could remember striving for her swimming goals. She'd put everything into it and shaped her world around it. She'd been driven and dedicated and *obsessed*, quite frankly. She'd had to be to get up at four-thirty each morning and head for the pool. To stare at that line on the bottom of the pool for lap after lap. To maintain the strict training regime and the diet and the lifestyle.

She'd known she wasn't as naturally talented as other swimmers, but she'd had the raw elements—the height, the shoulders, the legs—to propel her bloody fast through the water. But without quite the same intrinsic talent as her competitors she'd had to work harder. She'd rarely let her hair down. Rarely taken a day off.

Her life had revolved around swimming and her goal.

And now she needed something else to fill it.

Stroke, stroke, stroke, *breathe*. Stroke, stroke, stroke…

She looked up just prior to taking her next breath—and just about sank to the bottom of the ocean.

Ahead of her—within a handful of metres, basically in the middle of the South China Sea—was Grayson Manning.

Her lips must have dropped open because salty water filled her mouth, making her cough and splutter.

'Hey!' Gray said, swimming closer. 'Are you all right?'

He reached out towards her but Lanie shooed him away, treading water. 'Of course I'm fine,' she said.

She'd stopped her swim so abruptly that her hair half covered her eyes. Automatically she dipped beneath the water and then ran her hands through her hair as she resurfaced, so her hair was slicked back from her face.

The action had moved her closer to Gray—really close, actually. Close enough that she could see the water droplets on his eyelashes.

She'd meant to say something—something inane to fill

the slightly odd silence. But as she looked at him—treading water before her, with the remnants of the sun, making him squint in an unfairly attractive manner—she found herself swallowing her words instead.

And saying nothing at all.

Gray hadn't really thought too much about what he'd do once he swam out to Lanie. Just that it seemed the logical thing to do.

Lanie was swimming, he was surprised and curious about that fact, plus it was hot and he wanted to swim—so he'd swum out to her.

But now he was here he wasn't sure what to do next.

Right now his body seemed quite content just to stay here, simply *looking* at her.

When she'd done that thing—that neat little dive and elegant reappearance with her hair slicked away from her face in shades of dark blond and brown—it had been as if he was seeing his assistant for the first time.

There'd been moments, of course, when he'd noted Lanie's attractiveness. Her eyes he'd noticed immediately—right back at her interview. And then the first day she'd worn her hair tied back in a ponytail, rather than spilling forward and covering her face. He thought she'd changed her hair again the other week too—her hair framed her face rather than shrouding it. And she did have a nice face—a strong jaw, defined cheekbones and a long, fine nose.

But that was the thing—he'd noted these things and had thought them nice. That was it, no further consideration. But right now she looked a heck of a lot better than *nice*.

Her deep brown eyes seemed huge, set off perfectly by her lovely, lightly tanned skin and the hint of freckles across her nose. Without her hair as a distraction her face was revealed for what it was—striking, defined and different. She wasn't model-beautiful, but she was…*distinct.* Much more than pretty. Much, *much* more.

'I'm sorry I don't remember seeing you at the beach,' he said.

He hadn't planned to say that, and Lanie blinked at him for a moment.

'You swam out here to tell me that?' she asked, raising an eyebrow.

'Yes,' he said. Then, realising that wasn't true at all, added, 'No. Of course not.'

Lanie tilted her head, studying him as if he was a very, very strange sea creature.

He didn't even bother to explain.

'I didn't know you swam,' he said instead.

Her eyes widened dramatically. 'You didn't know I *swim?*'

He would have shrugged if it had been easier to do while treading water. 'How would I? We've already covered the fact that I've been oblivious to your presence at North Cottesloe beach for weeks, so I wouldn't expect me not knowing your extracurricular activities to be a surprise.'

Lanie's lips quirked up in a bemused-looking smile. 'Okay.'

They really were very close to each other. Lanie wore what he was pretty sure was a simple one-piece swimsuit, its practical looking shoulder straps visible above the waves.

'So you swim,' he said. 'What else do you do?'

'Is this *Get to Know your Employees Day* or something?'

Gray laughed. 'Not officially. Let's just say I meant it before. I'm sorry I didn't recognise you at the beach. It's not personal. I've been particularly…distracted these past few months.'

That last bit he hadn't meant to say at all.

But Lanie nodded. 'You spoke to me once, too. Before I started working for you. You weren't happy when I took too long to throw Luther's ball.' Her expression was unreadable as she waited for his response.

Gray grimaced. He didn't remember the incident specifically, but it sounded about right. 'I'm sorry about that, too.'

She nodded again, this time with a subtle smile. 'Thank you.' A pause. 'You were very grumpy that day.'

'I've been told I can be,' he said.

Lanie's smile broadened. 'Your sources are onto something.'

He couldn't help but grin back.

But then that slightly tense silence descended again. Water lapped against them both, making them bob up and down amongst waves that would not fully form until much closer to shore.

Gray caught Lanie's gaze, meaning to repeat his earlier question: *What else do you do?*

But she was still smiling, her eyes sparkling. She looked like—Gray didn't know what mermaids were supposed to look like, or water nymphs, or whatever, but he'd guess they looked like Lanie. Glistening with tiny droplets of water, she looked entirely natural in the ocean.

Much, much more than pretty.

His attention now was far from abstract. More so than even five minutes earlier.

He was looking at her not as his assistant but as a woman. Out here, both of them without the accoutrements of their roles—no suits, or laptops, or smart phones—it was impossible to think of her and of himself as anything but a man and a woman. It was all they could be out here.

Just a man and a woman. Alone.

Lanie's smile had fallen away and the sparkle in her eyes had shifted to something far more intense. Far more compelling.

One of them—her or him?—had moved a little closer.

He could see flecks of emerald in her eyes.

Something else he'd never noticed before.

As he watched she licked her lips, a bead of salt water dis-appearing with that little movement of her tongue.

Then, in a sudden splash of water, Lanie was not so close any more.

'Race you?' she said. Her voice was high-pitched.

'What?' He was trying to gather his thoughts, far from certain he had any idea *what* he'd just been thinking.

'Back to the beach.' Her voice was steadier now. She ges-tured parallel to the shore with one arm. 'Swim straight this way till we're in line with the lifeguard's chair, then first one out of the water wins.'

'And the winner gets…?' he prompted.

'I'll decide what I want later,' she said with a cocky grin.

Gray made a show of sizing her up. 'You sound extremely sure of yourself.'

Remarkably so. Sure, she could clearly swim, but he was taller and stronger.

'I am,' she said.

He considered offering her a head start but from the steely look in her gaze decided that would be a very bad idea. He guessed Lanie was the type of person who wasn't interested in winning any way but fair and square.

He could understand that.

'And if *I* win, I want—' he began.

'Doesn't matter!' Lanie said. 'You ready? Let's go!'

And just like that they were off.

He did better than she'd expected. Lanie had to give him that.

For the first half of the hundred-metre-odd swim he was her shadow.

But gradually—completely as she'd expected—she pulled away.

In fact by the time he emerged from the water in all his bare-chested glory she was already on her feet, hands on hips, waiting for him.

The sun was rapidly setting behind her and long shadows were thrown by the backdrop of towering palms. Gray walked in and out of these shadows as he moved towards her, water sluicing down his long, lean body.

Unlike that day in his office, this time Lanie properly looked. She looked at the heavily muscled width of his shoulders. At the defined—but not overly so—shape of his pectorals. The lightest sprinkling of dark chest hair. The ridges of his belly. The way his shorts clung very low on his hips.

He was gorgeous. She already knew that. She always had.

Her gaze travelled upwards again to meet his own.

He was looking at her as he had when they'd been treading water in the ocean. How to describe it? Maybe as the opposite of the way he usually looked at her—or rather the way he usually *didn't* look at her.

This look wasn't dismissive, or uninterested, or brief.

It was intense. Interested.

In what?

The same question had triggered their impromptu race. The race that had been supposed to clear her thoughts, to give her time to realise that she'd imagined whatever it was she'd seen in his gaze.

Standing here staring at him like this was not conducive to that goal.

She gave herself a mental shake before taking two steps towards Gray and holding out her right hand, as if they were meeting for the very first time.

'Elaine Smith,' she said, then added proudly, 'Retired Member of the Australian Swimming Team.'

'This is not what I expected,' Lanie said.

Gray paused in the narrow laneway. 'You said you wanted me to take you to my favourite place in Hoi An.'

Her prize for winning their race. Although he *had* pointed out that he felt he'd agreed to the race under false pretences.

She'd countered by mentioning that, had he bothered to read her CV when she applied for her job, he would have known exactly who he was swimming against.

Which was a good point.

Lanie smiled up at him. She wore a long, summery dress with thin straps that revealed sunkissed shoulders. 'I was imagining a temple. Or a view from a mountain. Or maybe a fancy pants restaurant.'

'So you're not the only one surprising people today?'

'I guess not.'

They *were* at a restaurant—although the word could only be used loosely.

At the end of a long lane—which itself stretched down from the main street of Hoi An town, about ten minutes' drive from the resort—was a collection of mismatched plastic chairs and metal tables. The lighting was provided by naked bulbs strung across the back of a pale yellow two-storey building with dark green shutters and a red-tiled roof that was about five hundred years old.

The contrast between the ancient and the new was stark, and should have been ugly. But somehow this place—completely packed with locals—wasn't ugly at all.

It was vibrant and authentic.

And, besides, the food was amazing.

Gray led Lanie to a spare table—no one greeted customers at a place like this—and then left her for a minute to pay. You also didn't get to order here, either.

As he walked back with a couple of cans of soft drink sold from a bucket full of ice, he watched Lanie, observing this place.

She looked relaxed, leaning back comfortably in her chair. Her gaze was flitting everywhere, as if she was trying to see and absorb everything: the details of the ancient houses that surrounded them, the raucous laughter from a table of Vietnamese women all dressed in modern Western clothes, the older woman who was yelling directions at the restaurant's staff as they ferried oversized tin or plastic plates to table after table.

He'd decided to come here without much thought, and really it wasn't the most logical choice. He'd meant for them both to eat dinner at the resort tonight, alone in their respective rooms, as he'd had plans to work late into the evening.

If he'd properly considered taking her out to dinner it wouldn't have been to this place. He would have taken her down to the banks of the Thu Bon river, where the streets on either side where lined with cafés and restaurants, all serving incredible food at tables located perfectly for hours spent watching the world go by.

Lanie smiled as he approached. 'This place is awesome,' she said. 'Like nothing at home.'

And instantly Gray was reassured. He'd been right to bring her here. She got it.

'Tourists don't come to this place,' he said. 'Quan, our driver, brought me here one night last year. It isn't the sort of place that appears in guidebooks, or in a glossy pamphlet at a hotel reception.'

'That's probably a good thing,' Lanie said as she poured her iced tea into a glass. 'If this morphed into a tourist trap it wouldn't be the same.' She took a sip of her drink and met his gaze over the rim of the glass. 'This way I feel like I'm in on a secret.'

Their food arrived—banh xeo: crispy deep-fried pancakes with a pork and mushroom filling baked into the batter. Gray showed Lanie how to add lettuce and roll the pancake before dipping it in a lime and chilli sauce.

He waited for her verdict as she took her first bite.

'Delicious!' she declared, and Gray felt as stupidly pleased as if he'd cooked the meal himself.

'I looked you up on the internet,' Gray said, after polishing off his first pancake. 'Elaine Smith, member of the Australian swimming team.'

Lanie met his gaze. 'And what did you learn?'

'That you were aiming for this year's championships.'

She nodded. 'That's correct.'

'And your sister is Sienna Smith.'

'So's that.'

Now she did break eye contact, her attention suddenly focussed on a stray beansprout she was twirling between her fingers.

'It must have been hard, watching her win after you missed out on the team.'

Lanie looked up and raised an eyebrow. 'You don't beat around, do you?'

He didn't bother to answer that question.

'That's not very sensitive of you, you know,' Lanie pointed out. 'Most people would assume that's a delicate subject for me.'

'Is it?'

Lanie shook her head, but said, 'Yes.' Then blinked, as if surprised by what she'd said.

But she didn't correct herself.

'Of course,' she continued, 'I'm absolutely thrilled for Sienna. It's amazing to see someone you love achieve their dream.'

'That sounds scripted.'

Lanie's eyes narrowed. 'I meant every word. What sort of person would I be if I didn't?'

'I didn't say you didn't. I'm just not sure why you mentioned it. We were talking about you, not your sister. I don't really care about what she did or didn't win.'

He reached for his can of drink, enjoying the play of emotions and reactions across Lanie's face. Shock, affront—and then careful consideration.

How had he not noticed how transparently expressive she was?

Well, the same way he'd not noticed that he'd hired a world class athlete. It was apparent such an oversight was not difficult for him.

'So you're saying it wouldn't bother you if I was insanely jealous, overwhelmingly frustrated and more than a little bitter that my baby sister—who only began swimming to copy me—has just gone ahead and done something I've spent my whole life dreaming about?'

'No,' he said.

Lanie gave a little huff of protest. 'Right. I—'

'I'd call you honest.'

Her mouth snapped shut.

She reached for her own glass and downed the remainder of the sparkling liquid in a single gulp. 'For the record,' she said eventually, 'I don't feel that way.' A long, telling, pause. 'Most of the time.'

Gray nodded. He believed her. 'Do you want to go for a walk?' he asked.

'Definitely,' Lanie said, already on her feet, as if keen to escape from the conversation as quickly as possible.

Minutes later they were heading down Le Loi Street, which stretched all the way down to the river. Red paper lanterns were strung across the street, and with motorbikes parked along the footpath the narrow street itself was full with foot traffic—only the occasional swift-moving bicycle or a motorbike heralding its arrival with a toot of its horn wove amongst the crowd.

It wasn't late, and many of the shops remained open. Each flung light across the street, and the walls of colourful fabrics inside drew tourists towards them like moths.

Lanie's walk had slowed almost to a standstill. 'Can I have a look?' she asked.

Gray nodded. Even he with his bulk-purchasing approach

to clothing had been attracted to the famous Hoi An cloth shops. Le Loi Street was almost entirely full of them—and this was far from the only street in Hoi An like this. From suits to shirts to evening gowns, tourists could have almost anything made to measure—generally overnight.

If he'd had more time on his fleeting business visits he might even have had a suit or two made. But he hadn't, and he definitely wouldn't have time this trip, either.

For the first time in hours—since he'd dived into the ocean, actually—the real reason for this trip rushed back to fill his brain.

Temporarily he'd felt as if he was on holiday. A tourist, not a businessman.

He'd followed Lanie into a shop, but now he turned and walked out the way he'd come.

Lanie ran her hand down the wall of neatly folded silks and satins. Here they were organised in shades from the palest pink to a blood-orange-red, and the textures beneath her fingertips varied from silkiest smooth to roughly textured to delicately, prettily embroidered.

The fabric covered all three internal walls of the small shop. Suiting fabrics—pinstripes, wool and houndstooth—were just across from her, but it was this pretty wall that interested her. It was funny, really, she'd never been a girly-girl, yet it was this rainbow wall of pastels that had drawn her from the street.

A young woman had approached her as soon as she'd stepped inside, her black hair shining beneath the bright shop lights. Now she followed Lanie with a thick file full of pages carefully torn from top-end fashion magazines. She kept flipping to a new page, pointing at some amazing dress and ensuring Lanie they could make it for her, saying how beautiful she would look in it.

Lanie tried to explain that she was just looking to little effect. She knew Gray's schedule for the weekend inside out, and there was *no* time for this—no matter how remarkably fast the tailors in Hoi An were.

Lanie smiled to herself. Her sister would think this hysterical—that *Lanie Smith* was disappointed she wouldn't have a chance to shop. Combined with her makeover expedition, she was practically a shopaholic!

But here—with this wall of fabrics and the stack of fashion books and files on the battered-looking wooden desk in the middle of the shop—there was a possibility that maybe she could get something made just for her. Something perfect and custom-made that would…

What?

That would make her beautiful?

Lanie's hand stilled on a roll of fabric and she realised she was digging her fingers into it—hard. Enough to tug it a little out of its shelf. The shop girl watched her warily, as if she was about to fling the defenceless fabric onto the floor.

'Sorry,' Lanie murmured.

She turned, searching for Gray. He'd been standing amongst the mannequins at the front of the shop, but now he was nowhere to be seen.

She strode outside, negotiating the parked motorcycles to stand in the middle of the street. Gray should be easy to spot—and he was, way down the street.

Now she didn't bother looking into each shop. Instead she walked far faster than the groups of turtle-slow tourists, her flat sandals slapping on the bitumen.

Gray stood outside a café, his entire attention on his phone. Behind him a blackboard sign proclaimed free wi-fi with any purchase and an untouched frosty colourful drink in his spare hand made it pretty easy to put two and two together.

'Gray?' she said.

He glanced up. Not a glance like earlier today, but the

type she was far more used to. The type that seemed to look straight through her.

It was so unexpected she took a step back.

'I need to get back to the resort,' he said, eyes still on his phone. 'I need to deal with this.'

They were supposed to be continuing their walk down to the river. He'd told her of oversized, giant *papier-mâché*-like sculptures that floated along its surface in the shapes of dragons and fish. And a market across the bridge entirely lit by thousands upon thousands of paper lanterns.

But she didn't bother mentioning it to him.

It was a timely reminder, really. A necessary one.

Gray was her boss and nothing more.

Whatever she'd thought had happened down at the beach clearly hadn't.

It was as silly and misguided as the idea that somehow just the right outfit could make Lanie Smith beautiful.

That was never, ever going to happen.

Just as Grayson Manning would never look at her as anything more than his personal assistant—who had used to be a swimmer, once.

CHAPTER EIGHT

GRAY WAS TENSE. Very tense.

Lanie sat at the end of a long table, her laptop set in front of her as she took notes.

There were no conference facilities at the resort, so one of the function rooms had been converted into a meeting room of sorts. Although—wisely, she thought—Gray had decided to leave the floor-to-ceiling windows uncovered. Subsequently there was no mistaking where they were, with a sweeping view over the pools all the way down to the gently swaying palm trees and the pristine private beach.

For the investors gathered around this table today there would be no forgetting that they were sitting amidst paradise.

The goal was that all of them would find it impossible not to buy a slice of it for their own—either as a private retreat and long-term investment or to visit a handful of times a year and rent out to the fabulously wealthy for the remainder.

It was what Gray did—invest in construction and development and then sell the completed properties. The Vietnam-based corporation with which he'd built this resort—necessary due to Vietnamese law—would retain ownership and management of the main hotel-style half of the complex, while it was the private villas Gray needed buyers for.

Lanie had kept an eye on the five groups of investors throughout the meeting—on the sharply suited couple who made absolutely no concession to the heat, through to the maxi-dressed, tattooed woman with crazy, curly red hair whom Lanie knew had made her fortune shrewdly on the stock market. She watched their gazes drawn back time and time again to the view—to the promise and the possibilities that Gray was spinning for them.

She reckoned two of the five groups were already ready to sign on the dotted line—no question. The others—particularly the suits and Raquel of the maxi-dress—needed more work.

That Gray could convince them she had no doubt. She'd seen him in action before—he was good. Very good.

But today…

He was tense. Definitely.

Gray abhorred the type of presentation in which someone talked at words on a wall or screen. Sure, he'd show short movies, or photos, or the occasional chart or whatever—but generally his skill was talking. That he genuinely believed in the property he sold—his 'product', so to speak—came over loud and clear to anyone who met him.

He was passionate about what he did. Lanie was sure that that alone sold many of Manning's properties.

So, as usual, he wasn't standing at the head of the room and presenting. He was sitting at the table, having a conversation with the investors and answering questions while cleverly weaving his sales pitch into everything he said. Occasionally he'd stand and walk over to the windows to draw further attention to the view, or he'd ask Lanie to hand out yet another glossy photograph, or the impressive projected rental return figures, or research on the estimated growth in tourism in Hoi An over the next five years.

He was as smooth and as polished as he always was.

But he was tense. It was subtle—very much so. When he stood and walked around the room Lanie could see the stiffness in his shoulders beneath his cream business shirt. When he answered pointed and at times abrupt questions he would pause just that little bit longer before responding. And today, rather than *I know* or *This will* he was saying *I believe* or *Expectations are.*

She hadn't really believed him when he'd told her last week that this trip was particularly important, and that was why she needed to accompany him. She'd figured they were basically throw-away words, because she knew at Manning *every* project was important—particularly from Gray's point of view.

But now she'd revised her opinion.

She didn't really understand. Based on her knowledge of Manning's financial state—admittedly gained more from osmosis than anything concrete—everything was going incredibly well. Manning had ridden the Western Australian mining boom over the past decade to remarkably profitable effect. The company had developed and sold the flashy head offices required by the mining conglomerates in the Perth CBD, and had also diversified to invest and build in the mining centres dotted across the state. With the boom, by all reports, now gradually dying down, this new push into tourism and South East Asia was somewhat of a risk, Lanie assumed, but as far as she was aware it was a calculated one.

Nothing Gray had said or done in the time she'd been working with him had ever indicated that the company was in trouble.

But today, for the first time, she wondered.

The meeting ended and Gray left with the group briefly—the resort chef was conducting a special Vietnamese cooking class for their guests. When he returned he closed the door behind him and Lanie watched as he let out a long breath—as if he'd been holding it for some time.

'What's wrong, Gray?'

She asked it automatically, without thinking.

Gray's gaze snapped up to meet hers. For a moment he

looked as if he was actually going to tell her—although maybe that was just wishful thinking.

Then his eyes went cold and flat.

'I have no idea what you're talking about,' he said.

Then, as if the exchange had never happened, he walked over silently, pulling one of the chairs away from the table to sit beside her.

He began talking, his attention on her laptop screen—certainly not on her—without any expression at all.

But every inch of his body radiated tension.

Not that Lanie had any intention of asking him about it again.

Gray knew he'd stuffed up with Lanie.

He walked along the path to her villa, rehearsing what to say. He wasn't getting very far.

She'd thrown him before. Her question—asked so matter-of-factly—had felt as if it had come from nowhere.

He'd told himself that this first day had gone well.

That he had nothing to worry about.

But then Lanie had asked her question...

No. That was unfair.

He'd known he'd been off since he'd left Perth. He'd just been refusing to acknowledge it.

It didn't mean it had come as any less of a shock that Lanie had noticed.

Had the table of investors noticed too? The possibility had floored him. Made him re-evaluate every moment of the day so far.

So, yes, he'd been rude to Lanie. He knew it.

But how to explain?

As if he could just come out with it: *You see, it turns out the reputation I've built over the past fifteen years isn't as rock-solid as I thought.*

It bothered him enough that *he* was bothered by all this.

That he clearly hadn't been able to shake off his frustration as completely as he'd intended.

Who cared that some of Manning's clients would apparently much rather his dad was still around?

It turned out *he* did.

He shouldn't be dealing with it at all.

So, no. He wasn't going to tell Lanie the truth.

But a simple apology wouldn't cut it either. It had become clear that his assistant was not about to nod and agree to everything any more.

And he needed her help tonight.

Gray jogged up the steps to the front door of Lanie's villa, but just as he raised his hand to knock it swung open.

Lanie stood before him in her one-piece bathers, towel in hand—and nothing else.

'Oh!' she said, taking a step back.

His gaze travelled down her body—he was male and breathing, after all—and confirmed that she looked equally amazing in her swimsuit today as she had yesterday.

Tall and athletic, with never-ending legs, she looked like the world class swimmer he now knew she was. One with subtle curves in all the right places and—his gaze made it back to her face—blush-red cheeks and a furious expression.

'What do you want?' she asked. Her tone was pure frost. 'I believe I've finished work for the day.'

The combination of a near naked Lanie and his lack of preparing anything reasonable to say meant he blurted his words out.

'How did you know something was wrong today?'

Instantly her eyes softened, but she crossed her arms across her chest, her towel hanging forgotten from one hand.

She raised an eyebrow, and what she was thinking was obvious: *Seriously?*

Gray ran a hand through his hair. 'If I was rude to you before, I'm sorry.'

Silence.

He tried again. 'I apologise for my behaviour earlier. You've been a huge help to me this trip, and it was unfair of me to lash out at you about something which is not your fault.'

Lanie raised her chin slightly. 'Better.'

Her arms had uncrossed, and now she was fiddling with the towel in her fingers. 'Do you want to go for a walk?' she asked.

Not particularly. But he wasn't about to quit while he was ahead. 'Sure.'

Lanie had hoped the addition of a summery dress over her bathers and swift exit from the too-cosy confines of her villa would help. She'd felt far too exposed—both literally and figuratively—in her swimsuit, and had figured the beach would give her the space—mental and physical—she needed.

It was only somewhat successful. Having a business conversation while half-naked and in what was effectively her bedroom was clearly not an optimum scenario. But likewise walking along China Beach with six feet two inches of Grayson Manning with his suit trousers rolled up and his dress shoes in his hand didn't feel anything like a meeting in his office back in Perth, either.

But still, it would have to do.

As usual, the beach was deserted. The lapping waves nearly brushed their bare feet and a gentle breeze ruffled the dense line of palm trees. The sting of the sun had lessened, but it was still warm against Lanie's skin.

Gray cleared his throat. 'Why did you ask if something was wrong today?'

It was obviously difficult for him to ask, and no less the second time around.

Part of her wanted to push—to make him tell her what was wrong first. She shot a glance at him as they walked side by side and noted the hard edge to his jaw, and the way his gaze was remaining steadfastly ahead.

No, he wasn't going to tell her.

'Well,' she said after a while, 'it wasn't any one obvious thing.'

Instantly she sensed Gray relax, and that reaction surprised her. What had he expected?

'I doubt anyone else noticed,' she continued, and now Gray's attention moved from something in the distance back to her. 'I've just watched you in so many meetings that the subtleties stood out for me.'

He nodded. 'Like what?'

So she explained.

At some point they both came to an unspoken agreement to stop walking, and sat in the shade beneath a palm tree, their legs stretched out in front of them.

Gray didn't interrupt as she spoke, and it didn't take all that long, really.

'Thanks,' Gray said when she'd finished.

They were both staring out at the ocean as the sun set behind them.

Lanie was making a move to stand up when Gray spoke again.

'It's about my father,' he said.

Lanie sat down again, looking directly at Gray. He'd gone tense once more, almost as if he was angry.

'Okay...' she said.

'You wanted to know,' he said, with an edge to his tone, as if she'd somehow forced it out of him.

She went to stand again. 'Don't do me any favours, Gray. You can tell me if you want. Or not. Up to you.'

He stood too, and in silence they headed back to the villas. Gray was walking much faster than before—big, generous strides. Certainly not leisurely.

Halfway back, he spoke again. 'My dad retired a few

months ago,' he said. 'For years he's been little more than a figurehead. He's been my mentor, I guess, but not active in negotiations or anything like that. So, logically, his official retirement shouldn't have made a difference to anything.'

'Has it?'

Gray came to a stop. He shoved both his hands into his pockets as he faced her. 'That's the stupid thing. It *hasn't*. At least I don't think so. Everything's fine. Manning's fine.' He seemed to realise something. 'Is that what you're worried about? Job security? There's nothing to worry about on that front.'

She should have been worried about her job, but no. She'd been worried about Gray.

Ha! How stupid. As if Gray would worry about *her*.

A memory of Gray's hand at the small of her back at the airport, and his concern that day when she'd tripped on the street, momentarily confused her. It was easier to think of Gray as her grumpy, unreasonable, thoughtless boss. Not the man who'd raced her to the beach, or who hadn't judged her when she'd revealed more than she'd meant to at dinner last night.

Certainly not the man who was talking to her so openly now.

It was disconcerting.

'It's good that Manning is okay,' she said. She blinked, trying to get her thoughts back in order.

Gray studied her for a long moment. 'It doesn't make any sense. If the business is okay, if I know what I'm doing, and if this particular project is no more of a risk than any other significant new venture for Manning, then *why on earth* am I second-guessing myself?'

Lanie met his gaze. 'Because you're human,' she said, echoing his words of the night before.

His attention flicked over her shoulder, maybe to the waves beyond.

She spoke carefully, not even sure herself what she was trying to say. 'It's difficult to be so directly compared to someone else. When your father retired it was natural that people would search for change. That they would judge you and weigh up your achievements against what had come before. You'll be benchmarked against him for a very long time.'

'Is that what people *really* do?' Gray said, a derisive edge to his tone.

Lanie shrugged and her gaze dropped to her feet.

'It doesn't matter if they do it or not. Maybe they don't. Probably they don't—not all of them, anyway.' She curled her toes in the sand. 'All that matters is that you *think* they do.'

The touch of Gray's fingers beneath her chin shocked her.

Slowly, he tilted her face up again, so she was looking straight at him. Into his eyes.

'Who are we talking about here?' he asked gently. Too gently.

She took a step back, annoyed. 'You. Me. Does it make any difference?'

His hand fell away. The sea breeze was cool against the skin he'd touched.

He started to walk again. Whatever had happened then—if it had been *a moment* or whatever—had clearly passed.

Lanie took a second to follow him, but he paused a few metres away to wait for her.

Together, they walked again, the quickening breeze whipping long strands of Lanie's hair out of its ponytail.

'So what do we do about it?' Gray asked at the base of the steps to Lanie's villa.

Lanie laughed out loud. 'I wish I knew.'

A moment later Gray followed suit, and they stood there laughing together about nothing really funny at all.

When they'd both gone silent again Lanie gestured towards her front door. 'I'd better get inside. Sort out some room service or something.'

In response, Gray looked at his watch. 'Damn, I lost track of time.' He looked up at Lanie. 'Can you be ready for dinner in fifteen minutes? We're having dinner in Hoi An town with the investors.'

Lanie grinned. *This* Gray she was comfortable with. 'So what you're saying is that you'd like me to accompany you to a business dinner tonight, *please?*'

He nodded, completely oblivious. 'Yes. I realised today that it would be good to have you there. I should've included you from the beginning.'

'Okay,' she said.

But Gray had already turned down her steps, never even considering she might decline.

'Don't be late!' he called out, not bothering to look over his shoulder.

And that was just so quintessentially Grayson Manning that Lanie was laughing again as she closed the door.

CHAPTER NINE

THAT NIGHT WAS the full moon festival in Hoi An town.

Gray explained the celebration as the group had dinner in a café overlooking the Thu Bon river. On the fourteenth day of the lunar month the streets of the ancient town were closed to motorised vehicles and the street and shop lights switched off. The result was a world lit only by lanterns and candle-light—and, of course, the light of the moon.

It was a night during which the locals celebrated their heritage, and Lanie and the investors all got to experience this first-hand, with a dragon dance on the street outside the open windows of the café: three young boys—one beneath the elaborate dragon's head, another as its body, and the third providing the beat with a makeshift drum.

Amongst the celebrations, and at this simple café where each meal cost only a few dollars, they were a million miles away from the luxurious resort where the investors had spent the day.

It was a beautiful spot. Across the river the ancient build-ings also housed restaurants, all with packed chairs and tables spilling out onto the street, dark except for the smattering of lanterns. The temperature was balmy but far from unpleas-ant, and the locals and tourists were out in earnest. A gentle buzz of happy chatter spread from the street to the shops and restaurants and back again.

Lanie thought Gray had chosen well. *This* was what Hoi

An was about for tourists—amazing, authentic Vietnamese food served in the ancient town without any airs or graces. As lovely as the beach and the five- and six-star hotels that were popping up along it were, it was Hoi An itself that had originally drawn people, and it was this town that would continue to do so. She'd been here two days, and that *this* was what it was all about was already clear to her.

Hopefully the group of investors would see that too.

After dinner a line of cyclos arrived to whisk them out of the ancient town to where three cars waited to drive them back to the hotel. Lanie had enjoyed her ride down to the river in the three-wheeled bicycle taxi, seated ahead of her driver between the front two wheels on a canopied bench seat padded in shiny red vinyl. One by one each investor climbed into their own cyclo and were driven away two abreast, so they could continue their conversations as they sped across the cobblestones.

Lanie and Gray had sat at opposite ends of the long table at dinner, Lanie's role simply being to keep the conversation going—especially with Raquel and another investor who was travelling alone. Unsurprisingly the evening hadn't been about business at all—a few cocktails and their guests had seemed to forget about work entirely.

Raquel grabbed Lanie's hand as she stepped into her cyclo. 'Thanks for a fun night,' she said, squeezing her hand. 'I've never had dinner with someone famous.'

Lanie laughed. 'Not quite famous.'

'Pfft!' the older woman said with a dismissive gesture. 'Famous enough for me!'

And then with a wave Raquel was on her way.

Lanie was still smiling as she turned back to the road, but it fell away when she realised how close she was standing to Gray. It was the closest they'd been all night—almost as close as they'd been that afternoon down at the beach.

Her skin goose-pimpled, even though it wasn't even close to cold.

Gray studied her steadily. His face was shadowed, but the full moon overhead and the lanterns that edged the street provided more than enough light for Lanie to see he was truly meeting her gaze.

'Famous?'

'Uh-huh,' Lanie said with a grin. 'Haven't you heard? Raquel thinks she might remember watching the women's relay final four years ago, and she might also have seen me on television. Therefore—apparently—I'm a star.'

'She's right,' Gray said, very matter-of-fact. 'You are.'

Then he immediately turned away to speak to the driver of the waiting cyclo.

Lanie blinked at his back for a moment or two, not quite sure what to say.

Tonight had been the first night in ages—months, even—that she'd really, truly enjoyed herself. Just as Raquel had said, it *had* been a fun night.

Of course amongst the plentiful food and drink her swimming career had come up in conversation. Lanie had forgotten how normal people reacted to it. To her family and friends—even in her old job—her achievements had long ago become part of the wallpaper. But Raquel had been impressed—seriously impressed. As had the others seated near them.

For a little while she had felt a like a star.

So she couldn't really tell Gray he was wrong.

'Lanie?'

Belatedly Lanie realised that only a single cyclo remained outside the restaurant.

'Are you walking back to the hotel?' she asked with a grin.

Gray smiled back—the first time she'd seen him do so all evening.

'No,' he said. 'That market I mentioned last night... We...'

a pause '...we ran out of time yesterday. But I think you'd like it.'

Lanie smiled again. 'Sure.'

He gestured at the cyclo for her to climb in.

'So you *are* walking, then?' Lanie asked, confused. 'I can walk with you. I don't—'

Gray shook his head. 'There's heaps of room,' he said. 'We can share a cyclo.'

Lanie took another look at the bicycle-like vehicle. It was admittedly slightly wider than the one she'd been driven in on. But still...

'Maybe for two *normal*-sized people.'

'Don't be stupid,' Gray said. 'Trust me—we'll fit.'

He neatly ended Lanie's protest by grabbing her hand and tugging her into the cyclo behind him. The driver started pedalling the instant they were seated, and for a few moments they were both silent as they turned off from the relatively busy road along the river to an empty back street.

Silent and...squished.

From shoulder to hip to toe they were pressed tight against each other. The skin of Gray's arm was hot against hers, and their knees bumped awkwardly with every jolt in the road.

And then Gray started laughing. Laughing so hard his whole body vibrated—and consequently so did Lanie's.

'So it turns out,' he managed eventually, 'we *don't* fit.'

It was impossible not to laugh with him.

Their detour took them past a street corner crowded with tourists. Amongst the throng a small band played traditional Vietnamese songs and women in beautiful sashed dresses danced with oversized fans that flicked and flickered in time with the music. As they headed back to the river Lanie began to relax just a little—or as much as was possible given their proximity.

After their laughter faded away they didn't talk for the remainder of their trip—although it wasn't an awkward silence.

Lanie had expected Gray to ask what she thought about the dinner. She'd definitely noticed a subtle difference—not so much in the stuff he couldn't control, as she'd still seen the hints of tension in his posture, but he'd shifted his language, reverting to the more confident phrasing that she was more familiar with.

But she was glad he didn't ask. It was nice to play tourist for just a little while.

She risked a glance in his direction.

His gaze was directed outside the cyclo at the many shop fronts and the boats moored along the river. In profile, Gray was every bit as handsome as he was from other angles. Although this close she noticed he wasn't quite as perfect as she'd suspected. His nose *wasn't* quite straight, and had the smallest bump near the bridge. His just-too-long hair had a couple of flecks of grey, and he'd even managed to miss a section while shaving. The tiny patch of stubble was unexpectedly endearing.

He must have sensed her attention because he turned to meet her gaze with a smile. Of course she smiled back.

It turned out that even now—when Gray's smiles were *almost* a regular occurrence—they had just as much impact on her. It was near Pavlovian—one smile from Gray and her insides went all gooey, with a dopey smile to match.

Of course she knew this wasn't a good thing. She'd told herself that many times—particularly in the past twenty-four hours and *especially* since he'd dragged her onto this cyclo. But what she needed to remember was that it was natural for the two of them to feel some sort of temporary closeness, given how much time they were spending together.

That was what this was. Nothing more.

The cyclo came to a stop at the base of a wide pedestrian bridge. On either side floated giant lantern-like sculptures—far taller than even herself—bobbing amidst the boats on the river. A tiger, a serpent, a fish and more—all glowing in shades of gold, red and green.

'Come on,' Gray said. 'We'll walk this last bit.'

He stepped out and then reached out a hand to help Lanie. Once she was standing, and while he asked the driver to wait for them, he kept right on holding her hand.

Lanie looked stupidly down at their joined hands, but let him tug her behind him as they crossed the bridge. His touch did such strange and crazy things to her. This was different from how she'd felt in the cyclo because—like down on the beach—she couldn't interpret it as anything but deliberate. Sensations fluttered in her belly that she really had no business feeling.

He was her boss, after all.

And he wasn't interested in her.

Are you sure?

More than once now she'd thought she'd seen something when he'd looked at her. As they'd swum together in the ocean. When he'd surprised her at her villa door in her bathers. That moment he'd raised her chin with a tender touch... And maybe now...

No. No, no, no, no, *no.*

She was being fanciful. Imagining things.

She should pull her hand away from his immediately.

But she didn't.

She wanted to kick herself for her weakness. What was she going to do next? Swoon at his feet?

They emerged from the crowd on the bridge to a wide expanse of road on the other side. As the crowd parted their destination was immediately obvious: the Night Market.

It was so beautiful that Lanie came to a sudden halt right in the middle of the street. Gray's hand dropped from hers, and with the removal of his touch he returned her capacity for speech.

'Wow!' she said. Which pretty much said it all.

'I thought you'd like it,' Gray said, looking pleased. 'Do you want to go explore?'

As if that question actually required an answer.

The market was small—only a single row of stalls, plus a line of freestanding carts and stands selling jewellery and souvenirs. But what it did have was an abundance, or even an overabundance, of light. Each and every stall sold lanterns— lanterns in silks and chiffon and lace and cotton and in every colour under the sun. And all were lit—rows and rows of them. Pendant shapes and diamonds, columns and spheres. Some with golden tassels, others without. Some delicately painted, others tiny and strung together on delicate strings.

All beautiful, all bright, all magical.

There was no other light in the market but that thrown by the lanterns—but it was enough. Lanie approached one stall and a woman immediately offered to make her a lantern on the spot, in any design she wanted. Any colour, any size, any painted decoration.

Lanie turned to Gray. 'I don't actually *need* a lantern...' she began.

Gray laughed. 'Neither do I. But I have two from here at home, in a cupboard somewhere.'

Once again he'd surprised her, and she found herself laughing back at him. 'Grayson Manning the impulse shopper?'

He slanted her a look. 'Do you honestly believe you're leaving here without a lantern?'

'Good point,' she said, and then embraced the inevitable by weighing up her many, many lantern options.

In the end she kept it simple—a sphere-shaped silk lantern in a blue that reminded her of the South China Sea, with today's date painted in delicate script at its base. What she'd do with it when she got home she had no idea—it wouldn't exactly blend in with her mother's décor. But of course that wasn't the point.

Directed to return in half an hour to collect her new lantern, Lanie took her time browsing the other stalls, exploring even more lanterns, plus jewellery, trinkets and silk fans. Tonight Gray didn't disappear. He didn't hover over her shoulder, either, but browsed the stalls with her, occasionally drawing her attention to the weird and the wonderful—like the unexpected discovery that one stall was selling, of all things, cheese graters.

Eventually they reached the edge of the Night Market. They stood together in a puddle of light thrown by the final stall's lanterns, both of them looking back the way they came.

'I read your CV,' Gray said out of the blue. 'I figured I should check for any other hidden talents I was unaware of.'

Lanie shifted her weight a little uncomfortably. 'Um...' she began. How to explain?

'For an elite athlete,' Gray went on, 'you've managed to squeeze a heck of a lot into your business career.'

Maybe she'd imagined his questioning tone, but regardless she needed to tell him. 'My CV—excluding the swimming part—is a little...uh...*creative.* A friend of mine made some adjustments without my knowledge.'

'So you lied to get your job?' he said. But his tone wasn't accusing.

'In a way...yes.'

A long pause. 'I should probably be pretty angry about that,' Gray said.

Lanie met his gaze, and even in the lantern light a sparkle was unmistakable. 'Probably,' she said. 'But you're not.'

He studied her. 'No.' A shrug. 'You're doing a great job. And you haven't quit. So that's in your favour.'

'I've heard you have an issue with people doing that.'

Gray sighed. 'Marilyn says I need to be nicer to my staff.'

'Marilyn is a very wise woman,' Lanie said. 'Although you *are* improving. You've been almost nice at least once this weekend.'

Actually, many more times than that.

'Have I—' Gray began, but then a couple with a huge, fancy-looking camera began talking to them in a language she didn't understand—although their hand gestures soon made their intentions clear. They wanted to take a photo down the length of the market and she and Gray were in the way.

So they stepped aside—around the side of the last stall and into almost darkness, with only a few lonely-looking lanterns hanging above their heads. The move had brought Gray closer to her—close enough that she needed to tip her head up to look at him.

'What was I saying?'

'Something about being nice,' she said.

'No, not that,' he said. 'Your CV. If all that experience isn't accurate, then what *have* you been doing for work? Or were you paid to swim?'

Lanie gave a brief laugh. 'No! Surprisingly, an unknown relay swimmer is *not* a target for lucrative sponsorship deals.' She briefly explained her old job at the swim-school, which she'd taken to support the limited government funding her swimming had received.

He looked at her curiously. 'Why are you working for me?'

'Because you're such a nice guy?' she said, trying another laugh. But this one was even less successful.

'No, I'm serious,' he said. 'Is this what you want? A career in business?'

Lanie wrapped her arms around her waist. Her stomach was feeling strangely empty, despite their recent meal. 'Why not?' she said.

Gray shook his head, and the small action made Lanie's jaw go tense.

'You're not young for a swimmer,' he said, oblivious to Lanie's narrowing eyes. 'So I'm guessing swimming has been your life for—what?—ten years?'

'Longer,' she said.

'So after all those years focusing on and striving for one

thing—being completely driven by your own goals and aspirations—you walk away to be my assistant?'

Lanie felt her nails digging into her waist. 'It was the right time for me to retire,' she said very tightly. 'And there's nothing wrong with being a personal assistant.'

'Of course not,' he said. 'If that's what you want.'

She couldn't listen to this. 'I don't have the luxury of *doing what I want*, Gray. Not many people do.'

Lanie didn't want to stand still any longer. She stepped away, needing to walk somewhere. Away from Gray.

But his hand, light on her upper arm, slowed her. Then his voice, quiet but firm, stilled her. 'What *do* you want, Lanie?'

She shrugged his touch away, not needing the distraction. Gray was standing directly below the small cluster of lanterns. Their light was inconsistent, putting his face into flickering shadow. She couldn't quite make out what she was seeing in his gaze—but she could guess.

Concern.

Pity.

'I wanted a gold medal, Gray,' she said. She spat the words out, as if it was a dirty secret. 'But you know what? I soon learnt not to be fussy. Then I just wanted a medal. Later it was enough to be on the team, to swim in a final. Then just being a heat swimmer was okay.' She paused, taking a step closer to Gray. 'I've got pretty good at downgrading my dreams. And how is it any of *your* business what my new dream is? Maybe I've just figured out that it's better to choose a dream I've got some hope of actually achieving.'

She dropped her gaze, staring at nothing over his shoulder. Somewhere at the back of mind she didn't understand her reaction. Wasn't this question exactly the one she'd pondered as she'd swum yesterday?

But then, maybe that was the problem. Yesterday she'd had no answers.

Today she still didn't.

She wasn't going to admit that to Gray.

She didn't even want to admit that to herself.

Gray shifted closer, and now the lantern light revealed his expression to her more clearly.

'Lanie…' he began, then paused.

If his gaze had held the pity she expected she would have walked away. If it had been compassion, or worry—everything she saw in Teagan's eyes and heard in Sienna's voice—she would have been gone. Out of there.

But it wasn't there. None of it was. He looked at her with… *something.* A mix of understanding and maybe respect?

Could you even *see* that in someone's eyes?

He reached for her again—this time for her hand. His fingers were warm and firm as they wrapped around hers.

'Don't do that,' she said, although she didn't pull away.

'Touch you?' he asked.

She nodded. 'You keep doing it. At the airport, the beach, just before…'

Lanie realised it sounded as if she'd burned every instance of his touch into her brain, and she felt a blush steal up her cheeks. He probably had no idea. It had probably all been subconscious actions—nothing to do with her.

'Why is that a problem?' His voice had become very, very low.

She was looking down again. At their joined hands. She had pretty big hands—they were in proportion with the rest of her—and long fingers. But Gray's made hers look normal.

Almost, but not quite, small.

'I can't concentrate when you do,' she said. And then immediately wanted to whisk those words away. She tried to make a joke. 'See? I don't know what I'm saying.'

But the atmosphere didn't lighten. If anything, the shadows in which they stood felt even more intimate.

Here at the end of the stalls there was no one. No tourists, no shopkeepers—nothing.

They were alone.

'Really?' he said. His grip shifted, moving a little way up her arm so his fingers brushed the sensitive skin of her inner wrist.

The tiny, delicate movement made her breath catch.

'You don't have to hold my hand, you know,' she said, her voice not sounding at all like her own. 'I'm not going to walk away. Not because you don't deserve it, but because I don't know how to get back to the hotel.'

Gray's lips quirked upwards.

'Maybe I'm not touching you for purely practical reasons,' he said.

Lanie didn't know what to say to that.

Her instinct was to argue. To say, *Don't be stupid.*

But as she looked up into his eyes, as she felt the gentle touch of his fingers and realised it was most definitely a caress, words failed her.

Electricity was shooting up her arm and her whole body felt warm. Different. Certainly not entirely her own as she felt herself sway towards him.

He was looking at her as he had in the ocean. With an intensity and a certainty that she didn't know how to handle.

She was familiar with a Gray who barely registered her existence. This Gray, who was making her feel as if she was all he was capable of looking at…whose gaze she felt travel from her eyes slowly, slowly to her lips…this Gray was completely overwhelming.

But, unlike that afternoon at the beach, she just couldn't make herself look away.

It was crazy. It was stupid. She wasn't even sure if they liked each other.

He'd moved closer. Close enough that she could feel his breath against her lips. Close enough for her to register that his breathing had quickened.

Had she done that?

His other hand reached out, but it wasn't gentle like the brush of his fingers against her wrist. No, his hand at her waist was firm and sure as it tugged her closer. A whisper away from their bodies touching.

It was as if he was impatient—as if he couldn't wait around for her to make up her mind about what was going to happen.

And it was *that*—that little glimmer of familiar Gray, exasperated, focused, impatient, *imperfect*—that shoved all the other thoughts and doubts from her mind.

Right here, right now, all that mattered was that she wanted to kiss him. Needed to.

And incredibly, remarkably—and unquestionably—he wanted the same thing.

She looked straight into his eyes and he must have seen what she was thinking. Instantly there was no longer any gap between them at all.

The touch of lips against hers was firm. There was no caution in his kiss. But then, would she expect anything less from Gray?

His hand slid from her waist to the small of her back, although Lanie hardly needed any encouragement to move even closer. Both her hands snaked up and around his neck, and her fingers into his too long hair.

She wasn't sure who deepened the kiss but it didn't really matter. All she knew was the brush of his tongue against her lips and then the amazing sensation of their tongues touching and tangling.

She leant into him, enjoying how broad and solid and *tall* he felt, needing to get closer to all that strength and warmth. His hands traced random patterns at her waist and then moved upwards to the bare skin at her upper back. There, his touch made her shiver—and wish that she had more of his own skin to explore than just the nape of his neck.

Lanie didn't know how long they kissed or how many times they broke apart to kiss at some other wonderfully perfect angle. It was a confident, passionate kiss, giving them both the time to explore each other's lips and tongue—and to experiment with kisses both soft and hard. And everything in between.

It was like no other kiss Lanie had ever experienced.

She'd never felt quite so involved in a kiss, never felt so focussed on the touch of mouth and hands. It was as if her whole world had narrowed down to this kiss, to this moment, and absolutely nothing else mattered.

Gray had pulled his lips from hers and was kissing his way along her jaw. The luscious sensation made her tremble and hold on tight as otherwise she had serious concerns her legs were incapable of holding her upright.

'Lanie?' Gray murmured against her skin.

'Mmm-hmm?'

'We should probably head back to the resort. I'm not one hundred percent on Vietnamese law, but I'm pretty sure if we stay here we'll be arrested.'

The words were light and casual, but they were enough to snap Lanie's eyes open.

She froze. Immediately in her line of vision was that poor, forgotten cluster of lanterns—at first a blurry mass of colour but, as reality rapidly descended, soon refocussed into sharp relief. For a moment she watched as they swayed in the evening air and the rest of her surroundings also rushed back into her awareness. The buzz of the market. Music playing, somewhere in the distance. And the almost silent swish of a bicycle along the street.

Oh, God.

Her fingers were still tangled in Gray's hair, and she was still pressed chest-to-chest to his body. She felt a hot blush accelerate up her chest as she yanked her hands away, but before she could step back Gray's grip hardened at her waist.

'Lanie?'

Keeping her eyes on those lanterns, she aimed for a tone

that was hopefully breezy and matter-of-fact. 'Now, we can't go getting arrested, can we? Wouldn't be good PR for the resort.'

More brittle than breezy. But it would have to do.

'No,' Gray said. For an instant his grip tightened again—but then he let her go entirely. Taking his own step away.

She should be relieved. It frustrated her that she wasn't.

She risked looking straight at him and he caught her gaze.

He watched her with questions in his eyes—questions she definitely had no intention of answering.

So she filled the silence before he could. 'We'd better head back to the resort. Busy day tomorrow.'

Gray nodded—a slightly awkward movement. Then he fished his phone out of his shorts pocket and led the way from the relative seclusion of the dark to the multi-coloured brightness of the market.

Lanie kept her gaze straight ahead as she followed him, just putting one foot in front of the other, trying not to think about *anything*.

But her body—her hormones or something—was determined to keep reminding her how she *felt*, and it took an effort to push all that away. She didn't want to remember how she'd felt in his arms. How she'd enjoyed the romantic flutter of his fingers against the skin of her shoulder almost as much as the more earthy, more blatant way he'd claimed her lips.

She wasn't doing too well on that front.

As they stepped back onto the bridge a woman ran up beside her, a sea-blue lantern in her hand. Automatically Lanie took it and thanked her, but she didn't really want the lantern any more.

Which should be unsurprising, given that Gray had so adeptly brought to her attention tonight that she had no idea what she wanted.

Except for a short while, in the darkness just beyond a wall of hundreds of rainbow-coloured lanterns, she'd definitely wanted Grayson Manning.

CHAPTER TEN

HE SHOULD HAVE SAID something in Vietnam.

Gray knew it. And he kept on knowing it with each painfully awkward conversation with Lanie back in Perth.

After their kiss beside the Night Market they'd travelled back to the resort in total silence. He'd studied her as she'd stared out of the window, trying to figure out what to do or say.

At the time the issue had been that what he'd wanted to do and what he'd known he should say were very different things.

Even in the back seat of that car, with Quan only metres away, the temptation to reach out and touch Lanie had been almost impossible to resist.

When they'd arrived back at the resort there'd been a moment when they'd both stepped out of the car and Gray had been sure Lanie had swayed towards him. He'd been sure that whatever barriers she'd built since their kiss were just going to fall away.

And even though he'd known exactly how wrong it was for him to want that to happen he *had* wanted it.

But then she'd given a little shake of her head—like a reminder to herself, maybe—and walked away.

Thankfully, somehow he'd had the presence of mind not to follow her.

But even so his behaviour had shocked him.

He was her boss.

Even his dad and his too-quick-to-love heart had never had an affair at *work*.

And to think he'd been so smug about his relationship history when compared to his father's: dotted with mutually convenient temporary relationships, but never, ever anything hinting towards permanency.

He'd decided long ago that marriage was not for him. His career was his life's focus—he didn't need or want anything else. No distractions, no loss of control, and certainly no risk of losing what he'd spent his whole life working towards.

Besides, he had no doubt that he'd inherited his dad's propensity for divorce. All he had to do was look at his track record with his staff—it was clear he did not do long-term well.

But apparently he did think it was okay to kiss his personal assistant. In public, no less.

Gray realised he'd read the same e-mail three times and was still yet to comprehend any of it—so he pushed his chair away from his desk, spinning it around so he faced his window, and the view down to the magnificent Swan River.

He should have said something in Vietnam. Or on the plane home. Or when they'd arrived in Perth.

So many opportunities and yet here they were—almost forty-eight hours after their kiss and he'd done nothing.

Except maybe subconsciously hope that the whole issue would just go away.

Kind of the way his memories of their kiss had so successfully gone away?

Hardly.

The opposite had happened, in fact.

Lanie Smith.

She was not like anyone he'd ever met…

She intrigued him.

And she'd understood that stuff about his dad—stuff he hadn't told another soul.

When he'd kissed her it had felt as if they'd been building up towards it. As if he'd been waiting for that moment. Wanting that moment.

And then, when they *had* kissed...

He hadn't cared about where they were, who he was or who she was. He hadn't cared about Manning, or the investors, or his dad, or his dad's new wife—or anything.

He'd just cared about kissing Lanie. And then, later, he'd just cared about getting her back to the resort and to his villa as quickly as possible.

But that hadn't gone so well.

He needed to talk to her.

As if on cue, an instant message from Lanie popped up on his computer screen.

Raquel would like to organise a meeting later today.

This was good—one of the potential investors for the Hoi An resort.

Great. Can you come into my office to organise a time?

Of course that didn't really make any sense—this was definitely a task more efficiently sorted by instant messages. But, well...no time like the present and all that...

His office door swung open and Lanie stepped inside.

She wore a simple outfit—a knee-length slim-fitting charcoal skirt and a pale blue shirt. She looked tall and elegant, with the shirt skimming her curves and her legs appearing to go on for ever. Having seen her in her swimsuit, he now knew they did. She also looked neat and professional, and the gaze she had trained in his direction—as if she was making herself look him dead in the eyes—was equally so.

It also revealed nothing.

She had a tablet in her hand, and she turned its screen to face him as she walked to his desk.

'You've got a few meetings already in your calendar today, but I think you can safely move this one.' She zoomed in on the appointment. 'Or otherwise—'

'Lanie,' he interrupted.

She watched him calmly. 'Yes? Do you have another suggestion?'

'I don't want to talk about the meeting,' he said.

'What would you like to talk about?' she said.

Again, very calmly. Although as he watched she shifted her weight awkwardly from foot to foot.

'I'll give you one guess,' he said.

Her eyes narrowed. 'I have no idea what you're referring to.'

'Don't play dumb. We both know what I mean.'

'And we've *both* been playing dumb very successfully, I thought,' she replied. Her attention flipped back to the tablet screen. 'So—'

This time Gray stood up, and Lanie went silent as he stepped around to her side of the desk.

'We need to talk about this.' He followed her lead and met her gaze—as if it really wasn't all that hard to be having this conversation. And as if his brain wasn't unhelpfully supplying unlimited memories of exactly how good Lanie had looked with her hair slicked back in the middle of the ocean.

Ha.

'Look, I'm not going to launch some sexual harassment suit, or anything, if that's what you're worried about. It was a mutual thing.'

The idea hadn't even occurred to him—although of course it should have.

What was wrong with him?

'No, that's not it. I just wanted to—' He searched for the right words. 'Clear the air.'

Well, that was lame.

'There's no need,' Lanie said. 'Don't stress. I haven't picked out a wedding dress or anything—I know it was a one-off, random thing. Two people travelling together, an exotic location…' She shrugged. 'It was a mistake. I get it. I know you'd never be interested in me in that way…*blah, blah, blah*…and there's the whole you being my boss issue…'

Her gaze had shifted now, to a spot just over his shoulder.

His instinct was to correct her. What did she mean she knew he'd never be interested *'in her that way'?*

She said it with such certainty—as if she truly believed that he would have kissed any random work colleague he'd been with that night.

The opposite was true.

'Lanie—' he began, then made himself stop.

What was he going to say? That in fact, *yes*, of *course* he was interested in her in *that* way?

Was he really? She was nothing like the women he usually dated. She didn't look like them, and she certainly didn't act like them.

And besides—what would be the point? He couldn't afford a distraction right now.

He remembered how she'd looked in the market, when he'd questioned her about why she was working for him and what she really wanted.

Her pain and frustration had been crystal-clear—and he hadn't believed her for a second when she'd spoken of downgrading her dreams. As if she'd accepted that fate.

She hadn't. She was still processing the death of her dream.

She didn't need a guy like him to come along and hurt her some more.

So, after far too long, he didn't say anything at all.

'Good!' Lanie said, all *faux*-cheerfully. 'Glad that's sorted. Now—can we work out this meeting?'

'So!' Teagan said over the top of her hot chocolate. 'How was Vietnam?'

'Beautiful,' Lanie said with a smile. 'Fantastic beaches, and Hoi An town is amazing. I'd love to go back one day.'

There. Well-rehearsed and executed, Lanie thought.

A waiter placed an oversized slice of carrot cake between them. They'd met at a café near Teagan's place in Claremont, just beside one of the area's trendy shopping districts. Outside, people flowed past in a steady stream, expensive-looking shopping bags swinging from their fingertips.

'And how was your prickly boss? I can't imagine he'd be much fun to travel with.'

'Actually,' Lanie said, 'he wasn't so bad.'

That wasn't quite to script. She'd intended to say he'd been as difficult as usual—and as he had, in fact, provided a few decent grumpy-Gray anecdotes she even had sufficient material to back that up.

She'd figured it couldn't hurt—Teagan didn't know Gray. What harm would it do to perpetuate the idea that he was the boss from hell?

'Really?' Teagan said, looking disappointed. 'Damn. I was imagining you wearing one of those pointy hats, cycling around Vietnam searching for the perfect triple shot latte or something else equally unreasonable.'

'That's very specific,' Lanie said, and Teagan grinned. 'But, no. Honestly, he's not so bad.'

Teagan's eyes widened instantly. 'Pardon me? Is this the same guy?'

Lanie knew she should stop the conversation, but just couldn't do it. 'I don't know. He was almost *nice* while we were away. Seemed to want to get to know me better.'

He'd been more than nice, actually.

'You mean like a real-life *normal* person?' Teagan said with a grin. 'Wow. Amazing.'

And then the conversation turned to the famous Hoi An tailors, and Gray—at least from Teagan's point of view—was forgotten.

Unfortunately for Lanie it wasn't so easy to move on.

Part of her—a *huge* part of her, actually—wanted to blurt

it all out. She wanted to walk Teagan through her weekend blow-by-blow, so that together they could analyse what on earth had actually happened.

It was what she and Teagan normally did. In fact they'd just deconstructed her friend's latest date.

It didn't feel right not to tell her—but she just couldn't do it. It was hard to tell with Teagan. She'd respond one of two ways: either she'd be really concerned—both about Lanie and Lanie's job—or she'd go right to the other end of the spectrum and tell her to go for it.

And, given her conversation with Gray today, neither scenario was relevant.

It was—as she'd said—sorted. Over. There was nothing to analyse: quite simply it had been a one-off that was never to be repeated.

A mistake.

'Sienna was in *Lipstick* magazine this week—did you see?' Teagan asked.

Lanie nodded. 'With that rower in Paris, wasn't she? She looked really happy.'

She'd looked beautiful, in fact, with her new boyfriend in posed photographs taken all over the French countryside. Blissfully happy in a vintage convertible. Effortlessly gorgeous on a picnic blanket beside a picture-book lake.

'When does she come home?'

Lanie did the maths in her head. 'In a few weeks. She's meeting Mum in Dubai and they're flying home together.'

Teagan pulled a face. 'So you get them both at once? Lucky you.'

She had to laugh. 'It won't be so bad.'

'Is that what you're telling yourself?'

'It helps,' she said, grinning. 'And I can't move out, so I don't exactly have a choice.'

'Why not?'

Lanie swirled the remnants of her cappuccino in the base

of her coffee cup. 'I'm pretty sure I'm going to go back to uni. Finish that degree.'

'Really?' Teagan all but clapped her hands with enthusiasm. 'That's wonderful!'

She raised an eyebrow. 'Am I really in that much of a rut?'

'Yes,' Teagan said seriously, then clapped her hand over her mouth. 'Well, you know what I mean. This current job is okay, but it doesn't really *fit* you, you know?'

'But it's a similar job to yours.'

Teagan waved her hands dismissively. 'My temping jobs are about raising cash for my Grand Adventure.'

Teagan always referenced her planned year-long trip around the world as if it were capitalised.

'They're just a means to an end.'

'But why can't *I* have that?' Lanie asked. 'Why does everyone—' She stopped, correcting herself. Now was not the time to think about Gray again. 'Why are *you* so sure I should be doing something else?'

'Because you're the most driven, most focussed, most determined person I know. Do you think an average person would've kept on swimming, kept on believing, when their baby sister came through and did it all so easily? That takes guts, Lanie.'

'Or stupidity.'

Teagan glared at her.

But, honestly, sometimes Lanie did wonder.

The next morning Lanie went for a swim.

It was still colder than it had been in Vietnam, so she wore her wetsuit. The truly dedicated ocean swimmers simply wore their bathers, but while Lanie admired their dedication she wasn't about to give it a go.

Stroke, stroke, stroke, *breathe*. Stroke, stroke, stroke, *breathe*.

Just as she had in the South China Sea, she let her mind drift.

Should she go back to uni? Or continue to work full-time? Maybe even finally make use of the deposit she'd been so carefully accumulating and get her own place?

Was *any* of that what she wanted?

Gray's question had echoed within her skull all week. *'What do you want, Lanie?'*

Now she let herself acknowledge her answer to that question: she didn't know.

And that was terrifying.

Today, certainly, she didn't have an answer. So instead she just did what she knew: she swam.

Stroke, stroke, stroke, *breathe*. Stroke, stroke, stroke, *breathe.*

She lost track of the number of laps she'd done along the beach—she just swam until her shoulders ached and her legs were no longer capable of kicking.

Knee-deep in the shallows as she headed for the shore, a familiar splash of red came barrelling towards her.

'Luther!'

The dog leapt about excitedly in the water, running up close to Lanie and then running away back to the shore, as if to show her the way to go.

Unfortunately it was Gray who stood on the sand and who Luther kept returning to.

So her original plan to ignore Gray should she see him down here—after all, it wasn't as if he'd notice her—was not exactly going to work.

'Hi,' she said, coming to a stop in front of him. She tugged her goggles off over her swim-cap and swung them absently against her wet-suited thigh.

'Hey,' he said.

He was looking straight at her—right into her eyes.

A part of her—a big part—was horribly aware that she wore no make-up, that she definitely had the imprint of her goggles still encircling her eyes and that *no one* looked good in a swim-cap. Meanwhile Gray, with his hair ruffled all over the place by a swift breeze, and in running shorts and a T-shirt soaked with sweat, still managed to look gorgeous.

It was incredibly annoying, and maybe that was the reason for the sharpness in her tone. 'So you've bothered to notice me today?'

Oh, no.

It was supposed to be a teasing joke, but it so, *so* wasn't. She'd sounded hurt. Upset. Not at all like a woman who'd completely moved on.

'I don't know how I ever didn't notice you before,' he said. His words were low and…intimate.

The way they immediately made her feel—the way they made her body react—didn't help her mood. 'Yes,' she agreed. 'I am a bit of a giant woman, aren't I? Difficult to miss.'

She pivoted on her heel, spotting her towel a few metres to the left of Gray.

'That isn't what I meant at all,' he said, following her. 'And you know it.'

She snatched up her towel and then realised this was generally the point when she'd unzip the top half of her wetsuit. Briefly she considered not doing so—but then, what did she care what Gray thought?

As casually as she could she unzipped her top, peeling it down to her waist. She'd worn her new violet bikini today, and strongly wished she hadn't.

She didn't bother responding to his last comment. She didn't fully understand her frustration—in fact she had no idea why she was standing here so wound up with tension.

Why was she angry at Gray?

She glanced at Gray, meaning to say something—something about not being at her best this early in the morning, maybe—when the way he was looking at her stole the words from her throat.

He was most definitely checking her out. And she was almost one hundred percent certain that he liked what he saw. The intensity of his attention—of his *appreciation*—was like a physical touch against her skin, warm and tingling. It skimmed across her from her hips, where the wetsuit hung low, to the indent of her waist and upwards, over the small-ish curves of her breasts.

And finally to her face.

His gaze locked with hers, and she saw that he knew that *she* knew what he'd been doing.

He shrugged without even the hint of an apology. 'I have no idea how I ever didn't notice you, Lanie Smith.'

Then he turned and with Luther trotting obediently beside him walked away.

'See you at work,' he called out, and the words were whipped away by the breeze.

CHAPTER ELEVEN

THE NEXT MORNING, when Gray ran with Luther along North Cottesloe beach, Lanie was there again.

As he ran he'd occasionally search for her in the water—looking for the rhythmic splash of her kicks and the elegant way her arms sliced through the water.

When she emerged from the ocean Luther spotted her immediately and sprinted across the sand and through the water to get to her as quickly as possible. Gray couldn't have stopped him, anyway—but he didn't even try. Instead he followed in Luther's footsteps, meeting Lanie just as she stepped across the line where the sand switched abruptly from soaked and grey to almost blindingly pristine dry and white.

'Hey,' he said.

Gray wasn't sure what to expect. Yesterday at work she'd done her ultra-professional thing and it had been as if they were seeing each other for the first time that day.

Definitely not as if he'd all but imprinted the image of Lanie in that amazing bikini onto his brain.

'Hi,' Lanie said eventually—quite softly, as if she wasn't really sure talking to him was that good an idea.

He knew how she felt.

'I received an e-mail late last night from Raquel,' he said. 'She wants one of the three-bedroom villas.'

He'd planned to tell her at work, not here, but the words had burst out.

Lanie's face broke into a wide, genuine smile. 'That's fantastic!'

'Yeah,' he said as they walked to her towel. 'A big relief, too.'

He hadn't understood how much until right this moment. And Lanie got that too. She knew how important this deal was to him, and pleasure in his success was reflected in her expression.

After Lanie had stripped out of her wetsuit—she wore her one-piece bathers today, Gray noted with some disappointment—she towelled off and pulled on a tracksuit. Together they walked up the beach to the street. Gray had Luther sit while he reattached his lead to the dog's collar and he saw Lanie wave to someone. He followed her gaze to the tired-looking beach café—empty this early in the morning—and the man with the shock of white hair who was waving back to Lanie as he wiped down a table.

'Bob's my biggest fan,' Lanie said, then grinned. 'Quite possibly my only fan, actually.'

And then, together, they walked up the road, talking about the new deal—until Lanie turned up her street and Gray and Luther kept on walking along the parade.

'See you at work,' Lanie said.

But at work the beach was never mentioned.

'My dad's new wife dropped by last night,' Gray said as they walked along the beach the next day.

Lanie hadn't been surprised to see Gray waiting for her on the shore when she'd emerged from the ocean. She didn't understand why he was, but she did know seeing him watching her walk through the waves made her smile. And for now that would have to do, because she'd discovered that thinking about Gray—about any of this—was far too confusing. She didn't understand it, and certainly didn't understand Gray.

Today their conversation had been about not much—a bit

about work, but mostly nothing too important or serious—and they'd both gradually relaxed. But Gray's tone had shifted at the mention of his father.

'New wife?'

Gray nodded. 'Number seven.'

'Seven! Do you have any brothers or sisters?'

He shook his head. 'No, I'm the only one—the result of marriage number two. It was the longest my father remained married—almost three years, actually.'

'Are you close to your mum?' Lanie asked.

'We're in touch occasionally, but we're not close. My dad was really my primary carer as I grew up. He was great—very hands-on—and he'd often drag me with him to work rather than hiring a nanny or sending me to childcare. Mum went back to Sydney, where she's from, after they split, although I saw her on school holidays.'

'When you were—what? Three?' Lanie asked, incredulous.

'Two,' Gray confirmed. 'As I said, we're not close.'

Lanie nodded, but was unable to imagine a mother walking away from a child that young. For all her own mother's flaws, Lanie knew her mum loved her.

But then she guessed her father had done exactly the same thing just a few years later.

'My dad worked away,' Lanie said. 'And then left for good when I was eleven. He didn't even bother to stay in touch.'

Gray slowed down his pace just a little as he turned to her. 'So you don't see him at all?'

'Not once since he left.'

The words were matter-of-fact, but it irritated Lanie that she still felt a faint kick in the guts as she spoke. Her dad wasn't worth worrying about, and certainly not worthy of any remnants of hurt and regret.

'That sucks.'

Lanie shrugged. 'Hey, at least he gave me these shoulders,'

she said, with a grin that she only had to force a little. 'So, the new wife came over…?'

'Yeah.' Gray rubbed his forehead. 'I don't get it. It happens every time. These women inexplicably feel the need to *connect* with me. To *know* me. When I know it's a total waste of time. This one will be gone in a year—guaranteed.'

Lanie snorted with laughter. 'Wow. I can't see at *all* why this poor woman is feeling insecure around you.'

Gray looked so surprised at her comment Lanie laughed some more. 'Oh, come on. I can just imagine how you'd be around her. Probably like you were with me at first.'

And how he still was, at times. Not down here at the beach but at work, where he got so caught up in what he was doing that her presence seemed to cease to register altogether.

He opened his mouth as if he was going to protest, but then stopped. 'Possibly,' he finally conceded.

Ahead of them Luther had found a friend—a small black poodle—and together they took turns chasing each other into the water.

'But what if this one—wife number seven—is, in fact, *the one*?' Lanie asked. 'Isn't it worth getting to know her just in case?'

Now Gray laughed. 'She's barely ten years older than me. It's not going to last. My dad's one flaw is his inability to be sensible around women. For such a successful, accomplished, intelligent guy, his stubborn faith in love is bizarre. In that way I'm nothing like him.'

Lanie smiled. 'I never would've guessed.'

The Manning office gossip had confirmed what Lanie had already guessed: Gray's previous relationships had been both short-lived and superficial. Since his father had retired the consensus was that he'd been seeing no one at all, so complete was his focus on work.

'I'm not sure I agree that being a success and believing in love are mutually exclusive things,' Lanie pointed out.

'Maybe they aren't for some people,' he said. 'But my dad has lost millions with each of his marriages. And yet he keeps going back for more.'

Lanie had never heard Gray criticise his father, but his scorn for his dad's romantic history was obvious.

'And has that caused him financial difficulty?'

'With his early marriages, yes—although he argues now that it was what spurred him on to diversify the business, to take risks. Because he needed the money.'

'So he's a risk-taker in life *and* in love?' Lanie said.

'Yeah.' Gray didn't sound so happy about it.

'I think that's nice.'

They'd almost reached Luther, who was busily digging a hole now his poodle friend had left with his owner.

'Really?' Gray said. 'You don't strike me as such a romantic.'

Lanie wasn't sure if she should be offended by that. 'I like the idea of love. Of marriage and a happy-ever-after.' She paused, trying to think how to phrase this. 'But I guess more in an abstract way. Something for other people to do, not me.'

'And why not you?'

Lanie laughed. 'My longest ever relationship was two months,' she said. 'I'm not much good at them.'

She said it lightly, although Gray's gaze still sharpened as he looked at her.

'I don't know, Lanie, I—'

Gray's words were cut off by a loud yelp.

Luther.

The dog was holding his paw in the air.

Instantly, they both broke into a run.

Gray dropped to his knees in the sand, reaching out gently to inspect Luther's paw. Immediately blood splashed onto Gray's arm—blood that hadn't been obvious against Luther's dark coat.

Lanie spotted the culprit—the dog had managed to dig up

a small pile of broken bottles that some thoughtless person had long ago buried.

'He's got shards stuck all over him,' Gray said, worry heavy in his voice.

'Take him to a vet,' Lanie said. 'I'll clean this up so other dogs don't do the same thing. And I'll cancel your meetings for today.'

Gray just nodded as he hoisted Luther up into his arms, his attention entirely on his dog.

Lanie watched as he ran up to the street, faster than she'd ever seen him run before despite the heavy weight he was carrying.

Then she laid out her towel and started piling it up with glass, piece by piece.

By the time Lanie drove up to Gray's front door she knew she'd made a mistake.

She'd questioned her decision to drop by on her way home from work more than once. Firstly when she'd gone shopping in her lunch break for a large rawhide bone for Luther.

At the time she'd figured it could wait—she would simply give the treat to Gray at work tomorrow. But then she wouldn't know how Luther was.

In which case calling him should have seemed the obvious option. Except she could just imagine how that phone call would go. Odds were she'd call at a particularly inconvenient time, Gray would be all distracted, and she'd be lucky to get a handful of words out of him.

So she'd told herself dropping by on the way home from work—especially as it was kind of on her way—seemed reasonable.

Until she'd actually been in her car on the way here.

Was she breaking the rules? Did they even *have* rules around their daily beach meetings?

She had no idea.

She glanced at the bone on her passenger seat, complete with a big red bow, and pulled herself together.

She was worried about Luther and had brought him a present. That was it. No more, no less. If Gray thought that was horribly inappropriate and it meant the end of whatever it was they were doing at the beach then so be it.

Maybe the beach thing was over now, anyway.

It was never going to last, their semi-friendship. Kind of like that one-off kiss. She should have known it was temporary right from the start.

Right. So. Yes. She was going to go to Gray's house and give Luther his bone.

She'd laughed at the analysis that had required her to get to that point at the time.

Now—at Gray's front door—her hesitation didn't seem so ridiculous after all.

This was a mistake. She shouldn't be here. Gray wouldn't want her here.

She knelt down in her slim-fitting trousers to leave the bone at the front door.

Maybe she'd send Gray a text to let him know she'd left it. Or ring the doorbell and then run away like some eleven-year-old playing a prank.

That idea—and the image of her running down Marine Parade in her heels—made her giggle. She was still giggling when the door swung open.

'Lanie?'

She looked up from where she was crouching on his doorstep—up long legs clad in faded jeans to his soft, ancient-looking T-shirt—to his bemused expression.

She shot to her feet. 'Oh!' she said. Then thrust out the bone she still held in his direction. 'I bought Luther a bone.'

'Thanks,' Gray said, and his lips kept quirking upwards, as if he was trying not to smile. 'Nice bow.'

'I thought so,' she said. 'Anyway, I didn't want to disturb you, so I'll just get going…'

'Do you want to see Luther?'

Lanie knew it was far from wise to stay any longer, and yet she found herself nodding enthusiastically. 'Yes, please. How is he?'

Gray held the door open for her, then followed her inside. 'He's okay. He needed some stitches, so he's a bit dopey from the anaesthetic, but he'll be as good as new in a few weeks' time.'

'That's excellent.'

Luther was curled up on a big cushion on the floor in Gray's lounge room. The huge windows showcased the rapidly setting sun and also provided an unobstructed view of the front porch. With the window's dark tinting on the outside she'd had no idea she was being watched. No wonder he'd been hiding a laugh—how long had she been dithering out there?

'Why didn't you knock?' he asked.

'I didn't want to bother you.'

'What if I don't mind being bothered?'

Lanie laughed. 'You hate being bothered.'

He shrugged. 'For you I'll make an exception.'

Suddenly uncomfortable, Lanie knelt down in front of Luther and scratched behind his long, floppy ears. He wore a large plastic cone to stop him licking his wounds, and looked most unhappy about the situation. 'Hey, buddy,' she said, low and soothing. 'You doing okay?'

Luther looked up at her with his gorgeous chocolate eyes and out of nowhere, Lanie felt her throat tighten.

What was she upset about? Luther, thank goodness, was going to be okay.

She stood up, walking briskly over to the kitchen to put some space between herself and Gray. 'Do you mind if I grab some water?' she asked.

Gray followed her—which wasn't part of the plan. So she moved to the opposite side of the bench as he found her a glass, needing that large slab of granite between them.

'I should've called you,' Gray said as he pushed her water across the counter top. 'Told you how he was.' He nodded in Luther's direction.

'No,' Lanie said, 'of course you shouldn't. You had Luther to worry about.'

He shook his head. 'I should've called you,' he repeated. 'I'm sorry.'

Lanie wrapped her fingers around the frosty glass. 'Okay,' she said. 'I'm glad you didn't come into work, though. I'm sure Luther appreciated it.'

Gray tilted his head back a little, as if he was suddenly intensely fascinated by his ceiling. He gave a short bark of laughter.

'That wasn't entirely why I didn't come in.' His gaze dropped to meet hers and he leant forward, gripping the edge of the granite with both hands. 'I didn't come in because I received *two* phone calls this morning while I was at the vet. Two more of the Hoi An potentials.' A pause. 'They're out.' He managed a humourless grin. 'Great timing, too.'

'Oh, Gray,' Lanie said, resisting the urge to go to him and…and *what*, exactly? She stayed put. 'I'm really surprised.'

'Me too,' he said. 'After Raquel signed up I thought I had it in the bag. That all that stuff we talked about in Vietnam really didn't matter—that nothing actually had changed since my dad retired.' He laughed again. 'That it was all in my head. Guess not.'

'It probably has nothing to do with you,' Lanie said. 'The investment just wasn't right for them.'

'What I do, Lanie, is target the right investors with the right projects at the right time. Those investors all had money to spend, and I'd hand-selected them. If the product was wrong for them that's *my* fault. If the weekend sales pitch was wrong for them, that's my fault too.' He walked to the fridge and grabbed a long-necked bottle of beer. Lanie watched as he twisted off the top and then just left the beer on the counter, as if he'd already changed his mind. 'So I stayed home this afternoon to mope with Luther.' He did that ugly grin again. 'Real professional of me.'

'I think you're being too tough on yourself,' Lanie said. 'I'm sure no one has a one hundred percent strike rate with this type of thing—not even your dad. You did your best. That's all you can do.'

His gaze jerked up to tangle with hers. Instantly she knew where this was going and took a step backwards before she'd even realised what she was doing.

'*Really,* Lanie? You think that doing your best is all that matters? I find that hard to believe.'

There was no point pretending she didn't understand what he meant.

Very deliberately, Lanie stepped forward again. 'I *did* do the best I could. I trained the hardest I could. I swam the best I could—my best time *ever* in the selection trials. I'm proud of what I achieved. That *is* all that matters.'

'You're right,' Gray said. 'Of course you're right. You should be incredibly proud of what you achieved—you *are* a champion. But I don't think you really believe that, do you?'

Lanie stared at her untouched water glass. 'I don't really think this is any of your business.'

'Why not?'

Her head jerked up. 'Because you're my boss and I'm your employee. This is all a bit personal, don't you think?'

All Lanie's sensible plans to remain on her side of the counter were ruined as Gray strode over to her. She crossed her arms, not about to back down.

'Is that all we are, Lanie?'

She nodded, very stiffly. 'Haven't we already covered this?'

'What are we doing at the beach each morning?'

Lanie shrugged. 'I swim. You run. We happen to do it at the same time.'

'Come on. That's crap and you know it. Why are you being so stubborn about this?'

Her eyes narrowed. 'I should get going.' She went to step around Gray. 'Bye, Luther,' she said.

But Gray grabbed her hand as she brushed past. 'Wait.'

She was right next to him and she twisted around to meet his gaze. 'Please don't touch me.'

He didn't loosen his grip one iota. But then she knew if she really wanted to pull away, she could. But she didn't.

She couldn't.

'Why can't I touch you?' Gray said, a dangerous glint to his slate-grey eyes. 'Because you can't concentrate? Why *is* that?'

Lanie glared at him. 'You know perfectly well what it is. You probably have women collapsing at your feet all the time. Don't act like you don't know the effect you have on women. You know *exactly* what you're doing.'

He took a step closer to her. Too close. But she felt frozen in place, incapable of doing anything but *looking* at him.

'Yes, I know what I'm doing,' Gray said, all soft and low. 'I can't speak for other women, but I have a pretty good idea what I do to *you*.'

Her body already felt hot, confused. Now an all-over mortified blush was added to the mix. Why did she have to be so transparent?

Finally her ability to use her limbs returned and she tugged her hand from his grip, taking a handful of steps away before turning to face him. 'What are you trying to prove? Just exactly how smug and arrogant you are?'

He walked towards her. Slow, deliberate steps.

'Has it ever occurred to you, Lanie Smith, that you have the same effect on me?'

All she could do was stare at him.

He took another step. Close enough to touch.

'I—' she began—but she really had no idea what to say. Her instinct was to deny—to shake her head and tell him that he was wrong, that this was unfair, that he didn't really mean that.

But would she actually believe what she was saying?

Did she really believe that incredible kiss at the Night Market had really been so one-sided? That their daily meetings at the beach were solely between work colleagues—or at a stretch, friends?

Or was it more that she hadn't wanted to acknowledge what was going on? That she didn't want to allow herself to consider—or hope—it was something more?

Because she knew she couldn't deal with another *no* right now. Another rejection. Another failure.

'What are we doing?' she managed eventually. 'What *is* this?'

Gray's lips quirked upwards. 'I have absolutely no idea. But right now I'd really like to kiss you.'

Well, when he put it like that...

What to do seemed obvious—the only thing possible. She reached for him blindly, her hand landing on his chest. Instantly his arms wrapped around her, pulling her close while he turned her, lifted her, and the next thing she knew she was sitting on the counter-top, Gray standing between her legs, her face cradled between his hands.

She'd never felt so delicate, so light—so sexy.

Then his mouth touched hers.

And just like at the Night Market suddenly it was as if this kiss was her whole world.

But this time there was no prelude, no preliminaries—it was immediately and completely desperate. He tasted delicious, fresh and clean, and he kissed her as if he'd been thinking about doing nothing else for weeks.

It was overwhelming—but also unbelievably good. With each and every kiss she felt her doubts flutter away.

That Gray was kissing *her*, that he wanted *her*, was obvious in every touch, every breath. His hands slid from her face to her waist, doing electric, shivery things to her insides as his hands moved upwards.

She had to get closer to him, had to feel his skin, and she tugged him closer, pushing his T-shirt up in messy handfuls of cotton.

His skin was hot beneath her palms—hot and firm and lean. He was kissing his way up her jaw to her throat and she heard his sharp intake of breath when she ran her fingernails along his spine. She gave a little laugh of surprise and felt his lips form a smile against her skin.

'Told you,' he said.

And she laughed again, before his hands, his mouth, just *him* swiftly converted it to a sigh. Then he was kissing her mouth again. And from then on that kiss—this night—was all that mattered.

CHAPTER TWELVE

'TELL ME ABOUT your swimming.'

Lanie turned on her side to face Gray in bed. He'd propped his head on his hand and his gaze traced over her shape beneath the bedsheet. Said sheet had dipped quite low on his side of the bed, and Lanie found herself distracted by how lovely all that naked skin looked in the soft light of Gray's bedside lamp.

She cleared her throat. 'Um...*that's* what you want to talk about right now?'

He grinned. 'It's not every night I have a swimming champion in my bed.'

'Former swimmer.'

'Oh, yeah,' he said, looking thoughtful. 'Good point. Come to think of it, I've had *many* former world-class athletes. It's easy to lose track with all those women collapsing at my feet.'

She shoved him in the chest, but ruined the effect by giggling.

'Hey—*your* words,' he said, then reached out to tug her on top of him as he rolled onto his back, so Lanie lay half on top of him.

She almost said something about her being far too heavy—but she stopped herself. Gray wouldn't listen. And besides, for once in her life she actually didn't feel all that big. In fact, she didn't think she'd ever felt more feminine. More pretty.

'So?' he prompted.

'What do you want to know?'

'How about you tell me what it's like to represent Australia.'

Lanie closed her eyes for a moment, thinking. It took a mental shift to refocus on her past successes. They seemed a lifetime ago.

'It's such a cliché,' she said. 'But, honestly, just being there was incredible. I wasn't expected to make the team—even six weeks before the trials I never thought I had a chance. I'd been unwell earlier in the year—a bad case of the flu—so even to make the team as a relay swimmer was a huge achievement. Then when I got there...'

She spoke for longer than she'd intended. Told him about her sense of anticipation before the relay heats, how the noise of the crowd had somehow drifted away as she'd stood on the blocks, waiting for the split second the previous swimmer touched the wall. How the whole meet had seemed surreal—even the weeks and months after.

Even now it felt as if that experience had happened to somebody else.

'It's an amazing thing you achieved—you do know that, right?'

Lanie caught Gray's gaze as he studied her face. 'Yeah,' she said honestly. 'I do know. No matter what else happens in my life, I'll always have that.'

'But you really wanted more.'

She blinked, surprised. 'Of course. At one point I had a chance of swimming in the women's hundred metres as well as the relay. I had a really good year. But then a couple of the younger girls caught up with me.' Lanie managed a casual laugh. 'As you mentioned once, I'm not all that young for a swimmer.'

'You're not old, either. Twenty-six, right?'

'Good internet searching,' she teased.

'Plenty of time for a new dream, then.'

Instantly Lanie went tense and rolled away from Gray to sit on the edge of the bed, her back to him. Her eyes scanned the room, trying to locate her clothing.

'Why do you do that?' he asked. 'Why can't you answer that question?'

'Why do you keep on asking it?'

Her shirt was just within arm's reach and she snatched it up, pulling it on over her shoulders in an awkward movement.

'Because the drive that got you so far doesn't just go away. No one trains that hard for so long without being a little bit obsessed.'

He paused. He wasn't telling her anything she didn't already know.

'I love my career,' Gray continued, 'and I love Manning even now, even when it isn't going as well as I'd like. I *need* it. I need that focus. It's different, but still I guess it's an obsession. I can't imagine not having it.'

It was on the tip of her tongue to argue. To tell him he was wrong, that it *was* completely different.

But maybe it wasn't. It seemed ridiculous that she and Gray could be similar in any way at all, but was it possible?

Lanie wasn't entirely convinced. Besides, he wasn't the first person to ask what she was going to do now. To want to know how she'd fill this new void in her life.

But he was the first person to persist when she didn't answer. The first person who seemed to *need* to know—as if it was incomprehensible to him that she could exist without a goal. Without a dream.

Because he knew that *he* couldn't.

So maybe they weren't so different after all.

With a sigh, she stilled her hands, her shirt still half unbuttoned. She twisted around to face Gray and pulled her knees back onto the mattress.

'I told a friend the other day that I was going to go back to uni. Finish a degree I started a few years ago.'

Gray nodded.

Lanie chewed on her bottom lip, knowing she could just leave it at that. She'd answered the question and now watching Gray watching her, she knew this time he wasn't going to push.

But he knew in a way Teagan hadn't that she wasn't all that sure going back to uni was the answer. It was clear in the way he looked at her. In the still lingering questions in his eyes.

'The thing is,' she said eventually, 'I don't know if that degree is what I really want. If it will lead me anywhere near where I want to go. Wherever that is.' There was a long, long pause. 'I don't know what I want at all.'

Her throat felt tight and she blinked away the prickling in her eyes as she crawled across the bed to Gray. He met her halfway and drew her into his arms.

Then she kissed him—because she desperately wanted to, and also because she didn't want him to see her cry.

The next day was Saturday, so they had breakfast at Bob's Café.

They didn't swim, or run, as Luther wasn't really up to either. Instead he curled up at Gray's feet, banging his cone-shaped collar on their chair-legs whenever he moved. It was warm, and they weren't alone in pretending it was already summer: the café was packed, as was the beach below them.

Bob came over with a menu, handing it to Lanie.

'Taking the weekend off?' he asked her.

She nodded, but Gray could see her smile was a little forced.

'I'll be back in the water on Monday,' she said.

'Good, good...' the old man muttered, then wandered away to take an order from another table.

Lanie leant back in her chair and propped the menu against the edge of the table. Her sunglasses-covered eyes were looking at Gray, and not at what they were going to have for breakfast.

'He doesn't give up,' she said. 'I don't get it.'

'Bob?' he prompted.

She nodded vigorously. 'First he was on about me swimming, and now that I am he's checking up on me. It's bizarre—like he's convinced I'm going to make some amazing swimming comeback or something.'

'Is that why he's asking?'

Lanie shrugged. 'Why else would he?'

Gray didn't know, but the man's persistence bothered him. Lanie wasn't going to swim competitively again. She'd made that clear. She certainly didn't need someone making her feel guilty about that, however well meaning.

'Do you mind if I ask?'

'Knock yourself out.'

A few minutes later Bob returned to take their orders.

'Lanie's retired,' Gray said, which wasn't exactly what he'd meant to say. There was an edge to his tone he also hadn't intended—but then, he'd never been known for his tactfulness.

The older man appeared unmoved. 'Yes, I'm aware of that.'

Lanie leant forward. 'And I'm not planning on competing again. When I swim now I'm not training. I'm just swimming.'

Bob turned to her. 'I know that too. So, what can I get you today?'

Lanie gave a little huff of frustration. 'Then why do you keep asking me about my swimming?'

For the first time Bob seemed to realise that Lanie was unhappy. There was a spare chair at their small table, and he pulled it out to sit down.

'It's simple, really, Lanie—you're a swimmer. A beautiful swimmer. You should swim. You're unhappy when you don't. I've seen you swim on TV before—I've seen the fire

in your eyes and the joy you take to the pool. When you quit
you were miserable.'

'I was miserable because I didn't make the team,' she clarified.

Bob shrugged. 'Possibly. But you're happier now you're
swimming again.' He stood up again. 'Now, what can I get
you?'

They ordered, and Gray studied Lanie as she sipped her
coffee.

'That was kind of weird,' she said. 'But kind of nice.'

'Anyone who's seen you swim can see where he's coming
from. You're something else in the water.'

A natural. His ocean nymph.

Gray smiled at such an uncharacteristically romantic idea.
Look what Lanie did to him.

'Do you feel like a swim?'

Lanie raised an eyebrow. 'What? Now? It must be almost
midnight. And,' she added, 'it's not exactly warm.'

The weather's premature attempt at summer had disappeared along with the setting sun. After breakfast they'd
walked leisurely along the beach with Luther, enjoying the
warmth and the salty breeze. Later they'd gone out to pick
up Thai food for dinner, and by then it had been cool enough
for Gray to wrap an arm over Lanie's shoulders as they'd returned to his car.

The action had surprised her—yet it had also felt somehow natural and almost normal.

Kind of like the entire weekend.

Now they sat together on one of Gray's soft leather sofas.
Lanie had her feet curled up beneath her and a half-finished
glass of wine in her hand. Gray was sprawled out beside her,
his feet propped up on an ottoman. Beneath the bridge of his
legs lay Luther, happily asleep and snoring softly.

'Why not? My pool's heated.'

Lanie grinned. '*Ooh,* fancy.'

'Only the best for Luther.'

She looked down at the slumbering dog. 'I don't think he's up for a swim.'

'No,' Gray agreed. 'And I can't say *he's* my preferred swimming companion tonight.'

His gaze caught hers and held—and its heat made Lanie's skin go hot, and somewhere low in her belly became liquid.

Lanie wondered if at some point she would get used to this. To her instant, visceral reaction to Gray.

Then he smiled at her.

A slow, sexy, smile.

No, she decided. She wouldn't—she couldn't.

Everything about Gray—the way he looked at her, the way he touched her, the sound of his voice—was almost too much. She'd never get used to it.

At the back of her mind a little voice niggled, attempting to remind her that she wouldn't get the chance to *get used* to Gray, anyway.

Lanie didn't know what this weekend was, but she did know that right now she couldn't think beyond it. And Gray certainly wasn't. They had tonight and tomorrow. That was it.

'I didn't bring my bathers,' Lanie said.

Another smile. 'I don't think that'll be a problem.'

The pool was deliciously warm.

Lanie swam its length under water, heading towards Gray's board-shorts-clad legs in the shallow end.

She surfaced beside him, standing. Her upper body cleared the water and her skin goosepimpled where it was exposed to the cool night air.

It was dark in Gray's garden, the only light coming from tiny uplights that glowed amongst the decking that surrounded the pool.

'You do realise you are very nearly naked in that get-up?' Gray asked. His gaze roamed over her—slowly enough to make her skin tingle.

Lanie glanced down at her underwear. She'd stopped at home earlier that day, so she was wearing her absolutely best lingerie—pale pink satin edged with white lace. Unfortunately at the time it hadn't occurred to her to grab her bathers, and underwear wasn't that great a substitute. As she'd expected, her bra clung to her like a second skin—and she didn't want to even *think* what the chlorine was doing to it.

'But I'm not naked,' Lanie said primly. 'I really do feel modesty is *quite* underrated these days.'

Gray's mouth curved upwards. 'Or,' he said, 'you're just chicken.'

Lanie sniffed deliberately. 'Well, I think I deserve a little more respect for showing some decorum—'

Her words ended on a shriek as Gray launched himself at her and they both ended up underwater. By the time they resurfaced Lanie was *sans* bra, and Gray held it aloft triumphantly.

Lanie couldn't help but grin back—especially as she realised it didn't bother her at all to be topless in front of Gray. How strange… Only minutes ago she'd almost lost her nerve while undressing beside the pool, but now—unexpectedly—it was okay.

Quite possibly Gray's *very* admiring gaze had something to do with it.

'You are gorgeous, Lanie Smith,' he said, soft and low.

Suddenly uncomfortable again, she automatically moved her arms to cover herself.

Gray's eyes narrowed. 'Don't,' he said.

'Gray, I'm not gorgeous—'

'Want to race?' he interrupted.

'What?'

'To the other end and back? Ready?' He didn't wait for her to reply. 'Go!'

He was off in a huge splash of water before she'd had a chance to register what was going on.

And because it was so ingrained in her she found herself swimming after him as fast as she could.

But even with a championship-quality tumble turn he still beat her back to the wall.

'I knew it!' he crowed, tongue firmly in cheek. 'That was just a lucky race in Vietnam.'

'How about we go again?' Lanie asked. 'This time both starting at the same time.'

Gray shrugged. 'I'd love to, but...'

'But?'

He grinned. 'This way we finish with me winning.'

Lanie laughed out loud.

But her laughter faded away to nothing when Gray stepped closer. He reached out to tuck a stray strand of soaked hair behind her ear.

'I like your hair like this,' he said.

'Wet, messy and knotty?' Lanie asked in disbelief. She reached up, patting at her hair ineffectually.

Gray's hand moved to still hers. 'Slicked back like this, so I can see your face properly.' He moved his hand from hers to trail a fingertip along her cheekbone, then down along her jaw. 'You have a lovely face.'

She shook her head unthinkingly and Gray's fingers slipped beneath her chin to still the movement. He tipped her chin upwards, so she was forced to meet his steely gaze.

'Let me say nice things to you, Lanie.'

She looked away, looked everywhere but at Gray—at the plants around the pool, the water surrounding them, then up at the moon.

But Gray still held her gently in place, and now he leant forward, his breath warm against the damp skin beneath her ear.

'I'm not making this stuff up, Lanie. I mean it.'

His words and his proximity made her shiver.

But not quite believe him.

And he knew. He sighed loudly in frustration. 'I'm not in the habit of lying.'

Lanie took a step backwards. 'You barely knew I existed until recently. Can you see how that might leave me a little unconvinced of your compliments now? From invisible to *lovely* or *gorgeous* is quite a jump.'

She could just process the idea that he was attracted to her, but the concept that she was anything approaching beautiful was a step too far.

'Lanie, I—'

She ignored him. 'You didn't even notice—'

She stopped, not liking the vulnerability in her tone.

'Notice what?'

She attempted a smile. 'My make-over. You know—new outfits, new hair, new make-up?'

Gray's forehead furrowed as he considered her words.

Suddenly Lanie wished she'd done as her mother had always taught her and simply thanked Gray for his compliment. She didn't even know what she was trying to achieve—did she actually want Gray to *agree* that, in fact, she wasn't even close to beautiful?

Really, there were far worse things to deal with than a man like Gray insisting on pretending she was something she wasn't.

'The day I asked you to come with me to Vietnam,' Gray said.

'Pardon me?'

His look was typical frustrated Grayson Manning. 'That was the first day you came to work after your make-over, or whatever. It was, wasn't it?'

Lanie nodded mutely.

'I thought so. Your hair was different. It reminded me of the day you tied it back for the first time. I remember I liked it.'

Another silent, incredulous nod.

He stepped forward, closing the gap between them again. He reached out, sliding a hand onto her hip beneath the water. Somehow she'd managed to forget her near naked state, but Gray's touch was an instant reminder. And now she didn't feel awkward or shy. Instead the soft breeze against her skin felt…amazing.

So did she.

'Why did you do it?' he asked softly. 'The make-over?'

'I was sick of being invisible,' Lanie said. 'And not just to you,' she added, only for the first time acknowledging that. 'But also in general. I've spent my whole life in my little sister's shadow.'

'You're not invisible, Lanie. I didn't pay as much attention as I should have, but I did notice you. Everything's been about Manning for me these past few months. It's all I think about it. It's all I do.' He paused, as if he'd just realised something surprising. 'Until now,' he said. 'Actually, ever since you argued with me about Vietnam.'

'Not agreeing with you instantly is *not* arguing,' she pointed out.

He shrugged his shoulders dismissively, but smiled. 'Since then, I can assure you, you've been far, far from invisible.'

His hand at her hip pulled her closer, then closer still, so she was pressed up against him, skin to skin.

She tilted her head upwards so their lips were only centimetres apart—but Gray didn't close that small gap.

'You're gorgeous, Lanie.'

He waited, her gaze caught in his.

'Thank you,' she said.

Then—finally—he kissed her.

* * *

They needed to talk about what was going to happen tomorrow at work.

Lanie knew that.

But she couldn't quite do it.

Of course neither of them had spoken about what was going on. Or about what was going to happen next.

All they had was this remarkable electric connection between them—but then, that was just physical attraction. Chemicals.

It didn't mean Gray wanted anything more from her than this weekend.

It didn't mean that *she* wanted anything more.

Did she?

They sat together on the balcony adjacent to Gray's bedroom. Dinner—a platter of cheeses and antipasto they'd thrown together—was on a small table, but they'd both stopped eating a while ago.

The sun was well on its way to dipping beneath the Indian Ocean's horizon. It was deep and red as it sank lower amongst the clouds it streaked in purples, oranges and gold.

Once the sun disappeared, *then* she'd talk to Gray.

But say what, exactly?

She had no idea.

Beneath them a cream-coloured, clearly extremely expensive sedan, turned into Gray's driveway.

Gray swore, and she raised an eyebrow in his direction.

'My dad,' he said in explanation, pulling himself to his feet.

And then, without another word, he walked back into his room. Moments later she could hear the thud of his feet on the stairs.

Lanie watched as a tall man—she would have instantly identified him as Gray's father anyway—opened the passenger side door for a delicate woman. She wore a polka-dot sundress, stacked platform heels and huge, oversized Hollywood sunglasses.

She looked exactly like the type of woman she'd expect *Gray* to date. Perfect, straight from the pages of a magazine—kind of the way Sienna was dressed in that Paris photoshoot, in fact.

Lanie looked down at herself. She'd only gone home briefly to grab some clothes, but her wardrobe didn't have anything like that woman's dress inside it regardless. She wore faded jeans, leather sandals and a loose camisole top. Very casual, very relaxed.

She'd felt good in what she was wearing. Thanks to Gray she'd felt good about everything she'd been wearing—or not—all weekend. Until about two minutes ago.

The front garden was now empty, and Lanie could hear the murmur of voices in the kitchen, followed by footsteps ascending the stairs.

'Lanie?'

Gray was standing at the doorway to his room and Lanie stood, stepping through the billowy curtains onto the thick carpet.

'My dad and his wife have surprised me with a home-made dinner.'

Gray sounded several notches below thrilled.

'Okay…'

And?

Lanie wished fervently that she'd got her act together earlier, or even that the sun had set faster. Then she would know what was going on—she'd know if Gray expected her to stay or if he wanted her to disappear into the distance.

As it was, she just felt terribly awkward. As if it was somehow her fault for being here.

She explored Gray's expression for some hint of what he was thinking.

But it was difficult. He wasn't even looking at her. Instead, he was looking past her—at the setting sun, maybe, or quite possibly at nothing at all.

Definitely not at *her*.

Lanie stiffened her shoulders. It had been so long since Gray had looked at her like this—or rather *not* looked at her, she'd forgotten how much it hurt. Or at least she'd thought she'd forgotten.

But just like that—just one dismissive glance—and she remembered. She remembered that first morning at the beach, when she'd felt invisible.

Last night he'd told her she was far from invisible.

Beautiful words she'd so pathetically wanted to hear.

But his glance now told her that was all they were—beautiful, *meaningless* words.

'Do you want to stay for dinner?' he asked.

She should have been pleased, but she wasn't. There was no question now about what Gray wanted her to do. And it *wasn't* to sit down for a cosy dinner with his family.

The simplest thing, probably the smartest, would have been to come up with some excuse for why she needed to go. Easier for her—she could pretend to be a breezy, fancy-free woman who had incredible weekend flings without a care in the world—and much, much easier for him. But she just couldn't.

'Do you want me to stay?'

She needed to hear him say it. She needed the answer to the question she should have asked hours ago: *What's going to happen tomorrow?*

Gray's gaze flicked to hers and held, and for once she wished he'd kept on looking out of the window. Because seeing him looking at her—truly looking at her when he spoke—meant she already knew the answer. And, stupidly, when she'd asked it she'd still held the smallest smidgen of useless hope.

'It's probably better if you go,' he said.

Lanie nodded.

There—she had her answer.

Tomorrow, nothing was going to happen. Because whatever they'd had, it was over.

She followed Gray out of the house, past the curious glances of Gray's father and his beautiful, perfect wife and out through the front door.

He didn't walk her to her car. He barely looked at her.

She was—once again—utterly and completely invisible.

He muttered something about work, but Lanie could barely hear a thing past the furious mix of anger and humiliation that powered through her veins.

Lanie considered skipping her morning swim the next day.

In fact lying in bed for as long as possible had very significant appeal.

But a mixture of things—Bob's words, partly, but mostly her own need to feel the drag of the ocean against her skin—hauled her from her bed. Earlier than normal, though. With luck, she'd be long gone before Gray made his way down to the beach. If he came down at all.

She didn't wear a wetsuit. The perfect almost-summery weather had persisted, although it was still far from warm this early in the morning. She thought maybe the full brunt of the cool water would help knock some sense into her.

Or something, anyway.

Stroke, stroke, *breathe*. Stroke, stroke, *breathe*.

It was her racing breathing pattern, and her stroke rate was well up. This wasn't a leisurely swim while she let her mind drift. She was powering through the water, slicing through it as fast as she could.

Every muscle in her body ached. She hadn't warmed up properly. She hadn't intended to swim like this—to swim this fast.

But she couldn't help herself. She needed to do this.

Needed to remind herself of the speed she was capable of. Of her power.

This she could control. She couldn't control the outcome of the team selection trials. She couldn't control the contrast between her sister's success and her own. She couldn't control whether Gray wanted more from her than a weekend. And it seemed she certainly couldn't control how she felt about that.

But she *could* control her body. She could harness the height and the strength she'd been born with, the years of training and perfecting her technique. She could swim, and swim brilliantly.

Her arms tangled in something and she came to an abrupt halt. She gasped, treading water, as she took a moment to register exactly what she'd swum into.

Seaweed—browny-green and curling. She pulled it from her arm, then rotated on the spot to look back towards North Cottesloe beach.

She was breathing heavily. She was far from race-fit and her body wasn't used to such punishment.

But, strangely she quite liked the ache in her lungs, the way her chest was heaving and the way her legs felt heavy as they moved in the water.

She felt alive. Wide awake. Not in that fog of hurt and anger she'd been existing in since she'd driven away from Gray's house last night.

She'd been so, *so* stupid.

As if Gray had *ever* suggested he wanted anything more from her than an opportunity for them both to explore the unexpected electricity between them.

He hadn't promised her anything. He hadn't even implied.

And yet she'd relaxed into his world with him over the weekend—she'd relaxed around *him*. She'd let down the walls that she'd so carefully built—walls intended to keep her from hurt just like this.

She was angry with him for the way he'd treated her last

night. But mostly she was angry at herself. She should never have allowed herself to be in that situation. It should never have happened.

She swam back to the shore much more slowly, taking her time and keeping her head above water as she swam leisurely breaststrokes. It seemed Bob was onto something, although today she couldn't say that swimming was making her happy.

But it helped.

CHAPTER THIRTEEN

JUST BEFORE NINE A.M., Lanie strode into his office.

He'd been there for hours, arriving even before sunrise. His theory had been that the familiarity of work would be a good distraction.

The fact he even needed a distraction bothered him. His time with Lanie was never going to be anything long-term, let alone permanent. He'd always known that, and he assumed Lanie had too.

He hadn't really planned on it being *quite* so short, but really it was for the best.

His father's raised eyebrows and blunt questions after Lanie had left only underlined that.

'Who is she?'

'A work colleague?'

'Not a girlfriend?'

'No.'

'You're sure?'

'Absolutely.'

At the time he'd answered his father's questions honestly.

She wasn't his girlfriend. But later he'd felt uncomfortable, as if he'd lied.

Which was just stupid.

Now he just needed to apologise to Lanie for the awkwardness of last night and for causing her rushed exit—and that would be that.

But he didn't really believe that. He had a pretty good idea what was going to happen. The odd thing was, he wasn't happy about it.

Lanie came right up to his desk. Onto it she dropped a brilliant white envelope, his name neatly typed on its front.

'My letter of resignation,' she said.

Yes, exactly as he'd expected.

'You don't have to do that.'

She laughed. 'Ah, I think I do, Gray. You made that pretty clear last night.'

He pushed his chair back and came around to her side of the desk. He could see her considering and then resisting an impulse to back away. She stood her ground, of course—it was what she did.

He could count on one hand the other people who stood up to him, but he liked it that she did. Really, *really* liked it.

She'd forced him to see her properly, to really notice her—and to want to understand her.

Over the weekend he'd begun to think that maybe he did.

Which was fanciful. A weekend plus a handful of walks along the beach was nothing. It was as silly a romantic notion as his imagining of Lanie as an ocean nymph.

That should have been the red flag—the flashing stop sign he'd needed. At the time he'd ignored the warnings. It had been his dad arriving with his head still in the sparkling, naïve clouds about Wife Number Seven that had finally galvanised him.

He wasn't about to get caught up in the moment the way his father was so apt to do. To extrapolate a simple weekend of fun into something much, much more. No way.

Especially now. Manning couldn't afford the risk.

'I mean it. Although of course I understand if you want to move on. But you're welcome to stay. I'm sure we can retain our professional relationship.'

Lanie snorted with laughter.

'Professional like how we kissed in Vietnam? Or, even better, how we spent most of the weekend naked in your bed? Yeah, that was *super*-professional.'

She was trying to brazen it out, but he didn't miss the pink hint to her cheeks.

He didn't know why he was trying to argue with her. She was right. Their working together was not a smart idea. Standing this close to her only made that reality more clear.

Despite how inappropriate it was to be thinking it right this second, all he wanted to do was reach out and touch her. To drag her into his arms and carry on as if yesterday evening had never happened. To take them back to those moments as she'd watched the sun set over the Indian Ocean and all he'd been watching was her.

'I believe my contract requires two weeks' notice,' she said, when he remained silent. 'I'll honour that, of course. I'm sure the agency will be able to find a suitable replacement in that time.'

Gray just nodded.

He tried to hold her gaze, tried to interpret what she was thinking. Usually it was easy—she had such a direct way of looking at him. Direct and open, as if all her thoughts and feelings were on display.

But this morning it was different. She wasn't looking straight at him. She was looking at a spot on his shirt, or over his shoulder. Not at him.

She turned on her heel to walk away, but he reached out, touched her arm.

Just enough to stop her rapid exit—then his hand fell away.

'I apologise for last night,' he said. 'I was very rude. I—'

'Don't worry about it,' she said with a dismissive wave of her hand. 'It's fine.' She laughed. 'I don't think our weekend was really an appropriate prelude to dinner with the in-laws, do you?'

She made their weekend sound...like what?

He couldn't argue with her. She made it sound exactly as it was—a bit of fun. A fling. A weekend. Nothing more.

'You've got nothing to apologise for, Gray. We both knew what we were getting into, and it was fun while it lasted. But I think we can both agree it's for the best that it's over. You're not interested in anything long-term. And I...' There was a long, long pause. She swallowed. 'We both know that my life is messy right now. I need to sort myself out, figure out where my life is taking me now I don't have a medal to reach for. You've actually helped me realise that. And you're right— this job is *not* where I should be. Especially now.'

He didn't want to believe her. She'd been upset last night. Angry.

As if he'd hurt her. But she spoke today as if she'd wanted nothing more than he had.

As if she agreed that it was for the best it was over almost before it started.

Did she mean it?

He gave himself a mental shake. Of course she did. And if she didn't what was he going to do? Would anything about the situation change?

Of course not. He knew he'd done the right thing. He should be glad that she agreed—that in fact he hadn't hurt her feelings the way he'd feared.

What sort of person would he be if he wasn't?

'You don't have to give notice,' Gray said. 'Actually, if you'd prefer, you can finish immediately.'

Lanie blinked and her mouth dropped open. 'But you have meetings all day, and I'm only halfway through that report—'

'I'll manage,' he said, cutting her off. 'Really. And I'll pay out your notice period, too, to give you a chance to find another job.'

She bristled. 'If I'm not working for you, you're not paying me.'

He shrugged. 'Then it's up to you.'

She chewed on her bottom lip.

'Okay. I'll finish up what I'm working on. It should only take a few hours.'

Then she nodded sharply, as if to confirm her decision, before finally walking out of his office.

After lunch Gray had a meeting across the city that ran well over time. By the time he returned Lanie was gone, her desk completely spotless.

It was for the best.

Teagan had arrived with a very large box of chocolates.

She thrust them at Lanie as she opened the door. 'I have no idea what this is about, but I thought calories and soft centres might help.'

'I'm sorry to worry you,' Lanie said. 'Honestly, it's not that big a deal…'

Her friend held up her phone to Lanie as they walked into the lounge room, her text message clearly displayed.

'Ahem…' she said, *'"Call me, please. I need to talk to you."* And no smiley face. So I knew it was serious.'

'I sent it at a low point of my day,' Lanie said. Just after she'd resigned. 'It was possibly over-dramatic.'

Teagan studied her sceptically. 'Right. Because you're *so* inclined towards hysterics.'

Lanie located a bottle-opener and went to work uncorking the Cabernet Sauvignon she'd picked up on the way home. When Teagan had called she'd asked her to come over after work instead. At the time she'd thought it would be easier than explaining the past few weeks over the phone. But now she had a sneaky suspicion she'd just been delaying talking about Gray.

But she did need to talk. She figured she'd just get it all out and then it would really be done. Over.

Although that was what she'd thought resigning would achieve.

Right in the middle of pouring the wine, Lanie found she couldn't wait any longer.

'I slept with Grayson Manning,' she said.

Teagan dropped the box of chocolates on the floor.

Most of the bottle of wine later, Lanie lay stretched out on her mother's overstuffed sofa, swirling the last of the wine in her glass. Across from her Teagan was sprawled in an armchair, her long legs overhanging the arm and swinging rhythmically to the sounds of late-night radio and the hits of a decade ago.

'You know,' Teagan said, 'I think this is a good thing.'

'How, exactly?'

Her friend turned her head on the chair's arm to look at her. 'I thought you needed to go out and have some fun. And I like that you finally did something even vaguely less than sensible.'

Lanie rolled her eyes. 'I slept with my boss, then quit my job without any other source of income.'

'See?' Teagan said. 'That's so unlike you. I like it.'

Lanie had to laugh.

'It's addictive, you know,' Teagan said. 'Doing impulsive things. Living your life in the moment.' She studied Lanie as if pondering something. 'It's a real pity you didn't get more than a weekend with this guy. Stretch the fun out a bit longer, you know?'

Lanie had told Teagan everything—almost.

She'd described the Night Market, their walks along the beach, that kiss on top of his kitchen bench...

But what she hadn't spoken about was the details. Their conversations. The sense she'd gotten sometimes that she was seeing a part of Grayson Manning that others didn't get to see—when he talked to her about his doubts, his father, or even his unusual view of relationships. And along with that came the knowledge that she had shared more with Gray then she'd shared with anyone—even Teagan.

He knew how to slide beneath her defences. He seemed to understand her. To *get* her. To push her buttons.

And she was different around him. It was ironic—the man who'd once made her feel invisible had triggered a...a quiet confidence, maybe. Definitely an edge. Gray's behaviour had pushed her to stand up for herself, to say what she was thinking.

To do what she wanted.

And where had that got her?

To her mum's lounge room, with a demolished box of chocolates and too much wine for a week night.

Gray sank back into his office chair. He didn't relax into it because he certainly wasn't relaxed. He more collapsed, actually.

Because that phone call had just made it official. He'd sold one villa—to Raquel—and that was it. The other investors were out.

Logically, he knew this wasn't a big deal. He'd had projects before that had been more of a slow burn. Others had sold in weeks, snapped up immediately. But then, this was something different for Manning. A new venture. He should expect progress to be slow. A delay was not a disaster. Yes, he had more capital than he'd like tied up in the resort. But they *would* sell. He did truly believe that. He needed to trust his instincts, to believe this development had been a savvy business decision. He'd entered a growing market at the right time. He would make money on this.

He did believe that.

But looking at the situation logically didn't make it any less frustrating. It didn't stop him from really, really needing some caffeine.

He leant forward again, lifting his hands above the keyboard to type out an instant message—but then paused. His new assistant was good. Über-efficient.

But really he was perfectly capable of getting his own coffee.

Besides, maybe a walk would do him good.

Was it the new venture? Or him?

Or, even better, a run.

It was mid-afternoon, so he hadn't really expected to see Lanie at the beach.

Still, he found himself scanning the waves for her, for that familiar way her body cut through the water.

She wasn't there, of course.

He ran hard, his feet leaving deep imprints in the wet sand as he propelled himself through the shallows.

He wanted to tell Lanie about what had happened today.

As he'd driven home he'd considered calling his dad instead.

But what was the point?

Gray already knew exactly what he'd tell him—and it would be no different to what he was already telling himself.

He just needed to carry on as he always had. To ride this wave and not let his frustration impact on the way he did business. Maybe it had in Vietnam, and the fact he'd allowed that possibility was infuriating. It couldn't and wouldn't happen again.

He hadn't changed. Manning hadn't changed. Eventually everyone would realise that.

He just wished they'd hurry up.

So, while his dad would understand, would be reassuring and say all the right things, going to him would feel as if he was doing exactly what many people seemed to think he'd always done: running to his dad for help. He hadn't done that and he wasn't going to start now. Gray *was* Manning now. On his decisions, his ideas, the company's success or failure rested.

So, no, he wasn't about to go running to his father. But he *did* want Lanie.

Not for business advice, or to tell him it was going to be okay—or anything meaningless like that. He wanted her because she understood this. She understood what it felt like to want something so badly and to be ultimately the only one in charge of your fate. When it came down to it, it had been just Lanie alone in that swim-lane. And it was Gray alone at Manning.

Gray's run slowed right down to a jog, then to a walk as he took big, heaving, breaths.

He looked out onto the ocean—out to the distance from shore where Lanie usually swam.

This beach was a world away from any aquadic stadium.

The kind of stadium she'd never return to.

For the first time the reality of that hit Gray.

All along he'd compared Lanie to himself. He'd sensed her passion, her drive to achieve. And he'd pushed her, unable to comprehend that a woman like her could be satisfied working for him. Could be satisfied without a new dream to chase.

But that was the thing. It was not possible to compare their dreams.

Here he was, furious with himself for a less than successful business transaction.

But he had another chance. Tomorrow. Next year. Next decade.

If he was stupid enough to lose everything, even to lose Manning, he could always start again.

There was no deadline on his dreams as long as he believed in them.

But Lanie…she didn't get another chance. She didn't get to go back and try again. To take a different tack, to review her training routine, to wring some non-existent bit of extra speed out of a body he was sure she'd honed to perfection.

She'd done everything right—her absolute best—and it hadn't been good enough.

She had to live with that. She had no other option.

And he'd been ignorant enough to push her. To question her. To think he was somehow helping by pointing out that she needed something new to strive for.

As if he had a Plan B for *his* dream. Manning was it. It was everything.

All he had.

His breathing had slowed to normal.

He should go home, have a shower. Maybe go back to work, or at least log into his e-mails from home.

He had lots of work to do. New projects to focus on. New investors to target.

But for once none of that excited him.

All he could think of was Lanie, swimming alone.

Lanie's mouth dropped open when she opened her front door.

'What are you doing here?'

A few weeks ago Gray had watched Lanie fidget outside his house as she over-thought how to leave her present for Luther.

Tonight Gray had done exactly the same thing. He still didn't know if this was a good idea—but it was too late now.

'I'm sorry,' he said.

Lanie raised her eyebrows. 'I know. You said so in your office. And, just like I said then, you have nothing to apologise for. I knew—'

'Of course I do,' he said. 'And you know it. I'm sorry for being such a bastard that night—because I was—but that isn't why I'm here.'

She crossed her arms and just looked at him, waiting.

'Can I come in?'

She shook her head. 'No.'

He took a deep breath, trying to organise his thoughts.

'I didn't get it,' he said. 'Actually, I *can't* get it. It's impossible for me to get it. And I'm sorry that I assumed I did.'

Lanie looked at him blankly. 'Pardon me?'

'Your swimming,' he said. Instantly Lanie tensed before his eyes. 'How you're feeling. What you should be doing now. I don't have a clue, and it wasn't my place to push you. To question you. I had no right, and I'm sorry.'

Her gaze had dropped to the wooden porch they were standing upon, but slowly she lifted her eyes until she met his.

'You weren't so wrong,' she said. 'You didn't ask me anything I wasn't asking myself.'

'That doesn't make it okay,' he said. 'You're strong enough to find your own new path.'

'I am,' she said with a slight smile. 'But you probably did speed things up a little. That's not a bad thing.'

There was a long pause. This was probably the point when he should leave, but he didn't.

'I miss the beach,' he said.

He didn't need to elaborate. She knew what he meant. Not the beach itself, but the two of them together there. Walking, talking. Laughing.

He could see her wavering, ready to deny him. Her eyes had narrowed and she'd taken a step forward, as if she was going to push him away physically as well as verbally.

But then, it was as if she deflated before his eyes.

'Me too,' she said. Then her gaze sharpened and she pasted on a plastic smile. 'But, hey, it was kind of fun while it lasted, right?'

'Does it have to end?' he said.

Her lips firmed into a thin line.

'You seriously want someone to walk with at the beach each morning?'

She was deliberately taking him literally, not making this easy for him at all.

But, really, could he blame her?

'I don't know what I want,' he said. 'I just know that I've wanted to tell you things—serious things, stupid things—I don't know how many times in the past weeks.'

Something softened in her gaze, but it was subtle, barely perceptible.

'And I know that I've wanted to touch you. To hold you. To kiss you. A hundred times more often.'

He was doing it again—tapping into this previously undiscovered romantic streak. It bothered him, made him uncomfortable—but not enough for him to wish back the words.

'What are you saying?' she asked. 'That you want more than a weekend together?'

'Yeah,' he said. 'More than a weekend.'

'And…'

'That's it,' he said honestly. 'That's as far as I've got.'

He knew it wasn't much, but it was all he had right now.

Her arms had dropped to her sides and she took a step forward. Then she seemed to think better of it.

'So you're saying we should live in the moment? Keep on doing this together for as long as it lasts?'

He nodded.

'That's pretty vague, you know.'

He did.

But then she took another step forward and reached out, touching his hand. He watched as she traced her fingers upwards, along his arm, up his bicep to his shoulder, then, finally curled them behind his neck.

She was close to him now. So close he could barely think.

She stood on tiptoes, her breath warm against his cheek.

'Okay,' she said, incredibly softly.

And he knew instinctively that even Lanie hadn't been sure what she was going to say right up until that moment.

That was how fleeting this was—whatever it was they had.

It wasn't a good idea. They both knew that.

But kissing her now, beneath the light of her front porch,

was the best idea he'd had in weeks. As was picking her up in her arms, despite her immediate half-hearted protest that she was far too heavy, and carrying her inside.

CHAPTER FOURTEEN

SOFT CONVERSATION DRIFTED into Lanie's subconscious.

Voices—women's voices.

She rolled over in her narrow bed and in her half-asleep state found that odd.

A few hours ago she'd definitely not been able to roll over so easily. Instead she'd been rather pleasantly squished up beside Gray.

But clearly he was no longer in her bed.

Lanie's eyes blinked open.

It was still dark in the room—not even a pre-dawn darkness, but proper, middle-of-the-night black.

She reached out blindly with one hand to turn on her bedside lamp, then flopped back against her pillow. In the corner of the ceiling hung the ocean-blue lantern she'd had made in Hoi An and she stared at it sleepily, thinking.

So Gray hadn't stayed the night.

Maybe that was how this new 'living in the moment' thing was going to work.

Lanie didn't know how she felt about that. She didn't know how she felt about the whole thing, actually.

But—no. Wait.

That was Gray's voice she heard. In the kitchen.

Lanie sat up, suddenly wide awake.

That *was* Gray's voice in the kitchen. Talking to her mum. And her sister.

Oh, no...

She leapt to her feet, fumbling about for a shirt to pull on. Moments later she was all but running down the hallway.

And there, in the kitchen, was Gray—in boxer shorts only, a hip propped against the benchtop. Across from him, perched on barstools, were Sienna and Lanie's mother. A small mountain of luggage sat waiting in the lounge room beyond.

'I didn't realise you were back today,' Lanie managed. She'd been sure it was tomorrow—although, to be honest, she hadn't paid too much attention. With an early-morning arrival, she'd just assumed she'd wake up one day this week with Sienna and her mum home again.

And of course that day was today—the night Gray was here.

She should have been more careful—but then, last night had hardly been planned.

'We guessed that,' Sienna was saying, with a very pointed look in Gray's direction.

'I thought someone was breaking in,' Gray explained, 'and then realised that was unlikely with their own key.'

Sienna laughed prettily, tossing her blond hair over her shoulders. For a woman who had just been on a plane for twenty-four hours or more, she looked remarkably well rested. And as beautiful as always.

Grey smiled back—men always did around Sienna—but then excused himself to get dressed.

The instant he'd left the room the questions started.

'Lanie, surely you aren't...?'

'Is he your *boyfriend*?'

'Who *is* he?'

Their surprise, shock and disbelief were obvious. And seriously unflattering.

'He's a friend,' she said quickly as Gray returned to the room. Now fully dressed, in jeans and a T-shirt, he was no less attractive than the boxer-shorted Gray.

To keep herself busy Lanie started to fuss around the kitchen making tea, while Gray answered Sandra and Sienna's questions.

He was doing well, really, given he clearly didn't want to be there. Lanie didn't want him to be here, either—this reality of Gray, her mum and her sister together was not one Lanie had ever expected to experience.

Gray said little. He didn't need to. The two other women filled all the spare conversation space and more. Lanie remained off to the side, watching them as she sipped at tea she didn't really want. Sienna was in her usual fine, flirtatious form—that was just who she was. Lanie knew it wasn't anything more than that, but still it irritated her.

And then Sienna brought out her medals.

As they were fished out of her sister's handbag and placed carefully in their boxes on the counter, Gray took a step towards Lanie, but she shook her head subtly. *No.*

Before she removed the lids Sienna's hand stilled and she met Lanie's gaze.

Lanie saw concern there. Hesitation.

But she also saw a mixture of excitement and pride—as if her little sister couldn't wait to show them to her. As if she was desperate for the praise of her big sister.

Lanie had never considered flying to London to watch Sienna swim. At the time she just *couldn't*. And she hadn't regretted it—until now.

Now she wished she'd been there to see these medals the day Sienna had won them.

Lanie smiled—a small smile that became broader when Sienna let out a breath she must have been holding.

Immediately Sienna reached for the boxes, and soon the medals were shining brilliantly beneath the kitchen's downlights.

They were beautiful, and far bigger than Lanie expected. She couldn't help but walk over, reach out and lift one from its padded bed. She weighed it in her hands and ran her thumb over the embossed surface.

Sienna was watching her with a worried expression. So was her mother—and Gray.

But there was no need.

That these medals were Sienna's—the result of *her* work, and *her* dreams and *her* achievements—was clear.

These medals weren't about Lanie. Not about her disappointment, or about what would have, might have…could never have been.

With a medal still in her hand, she went to Sienna, wrapped her arms around her and held her tight.

'I'm so proud of you,' she whispered.

And it was as simple as that. It was all that mattered.

Lanie walked Gray to his car. It was about two in the morning, but the idea of Gray returning to her tiny bed now her mother and sister were home seemed ludicrous.

It was perfectly still—still enough that Lanie could just hear the sounds of the ocean at the end of the road. She'd pulled on a pair of jeans, but now wrapped her arms around her body against the cool edge in the salty air.

'You okay?' Gray asked.

Lanie smiled. 'Yeah,' she said. 'I am.'

Gray reached for her, but she made herself step away.

'Lanie?'

She shook her head. 'I don't think it's a good idea,' she said. 'This. Us. Whatever it is.'

She had to push the words past her lips.

'Why not?'

Her gaze flipped up to the streetlight a few metres away. Its brightness made her blink as she stared at it.

'I think I've spent enough time in the past few months focussing on the wrong things. On my failures, my disappointments.'

'You're no failure, Lanie,' Gray said, his tone definite. 'Don't say that.'

'I know,' she said with a smile. 'I'm getting that now.' And Gray had played a big part in that—more than he'd ever know. 'I *did* fall short of my goals, and that hurts. A lot. But I need to move on.'

He nodded, letting her explain.

'The thing is, Gray, I don't think I can handle another failure right now. At least I can't handle one that's guaranteed. I need to believe in myself again.' She swallowed. 'So I can't do this with you. It's not going to work. We both know that.'

'But what do you want from this?' he asked. 'How can you be so sure it's going to fail?'

She laughed, but sadly. 'Of course it's going to fail. You can't even articulate what you want—neither of us can. But I know what you *don't* want. You don't want love, and you don't want for ever.'

She gave him a second—a moment to contradict her—but he remained silent.

She bit her lip, angry that her throat felt tight.

'That's what you want, Lanie? Love?'

Stupidly, she hadn't really considered the word in relation to herself. She'd just known that Gray didn't want it and had focussed on that.

But of course it was what she wanted. She turned her gaze back to him, looking him straight in the eye.

She had an awful feeling that love was something she already felt.

Could he see that in her gaze? She thought so, because his eyes drifted away.

'I think I get it now,' she said. 'That dismissive thing you do. I thought you were rude, or arrogant, but it isn't that, is it? You want to keep your distance from people. If you don't engage they can't get too close. Then there's no risk of any type of distraction—from Manning, and from your goals.'

He looked at her now, his gaze hard. 'You don't know what you're talking about.'

'I think I do, actually,' she said. 'I think for years I've been doing the same thing. My life was all about swimming—training, competing, day after day. There was no space left for anything else, and I didn't want anything else. But,' she said, with a smile, 'the good thing is that *now* I do have space. I have space for new dreams, new goals, new experiences, new relationships—and, I guess, for love.'

She'd only realised this as she'd been speaking. For the first time in months it was as if a whole new world was opening up before her—full of opportunities far beyond her swimming career.

Adrenalin pumped through her veins. Excitement.

Sienna's medals had been the catalyst, but this had started long before. Maybe that day she'd first stood up to Gray. Or when she'd finally believed in the way his body responded to hers. New emotions. New reactions.

Gray was shaking his head. 'You're wrong, you know. My whole career is about building relationships.'

'*Working* relationships, Gray. Not real ones.'

He laughed. 'Like my dad's marriages? Right. Or my mum's relationship with me? Or yours with your father, even? If that's what real relationships are, I don't want a part of one.'

Which was it, exactly.

Her gaze lifted to that streetlight again. She was discovering that right at this moment she was more like Gray than she'd realised. She couldn't look at him. Not now.

'Goodbye, Gray. This was fun while it lasted.'

He opened his mouth as if he was going to say something. But then he didn't.

Instead he looked at her—*really* looked at her—in a way that made Lanie wish she could take back everything she'd said. That made her want to throw herself at him and hold him and kiss him, take whatever it was he *could* offer for as long or as little time as he could.

There was passion and connection and maybe even something else in Gray's gaze.

But it wasn't enough.

She needed more now. A lot more.

And Gray wasn't capable of giving her what she needed. Or at least he didn't believe he was—and that was exactly the same thing.

He'd not contradicted her. He'd not even said he was willing to give it a try.

He was letting her end this and he was going to walk away.

That told her everything she needed to know.

So she let him.

One month later

It was a Friday night in an inner city pub, and Gray had met his dad for a drink. It was a celebration of sorts—three months since Gordon's retirement.

Gray couldn't say that everything at Manning, or his relationships with his clients and investors, was one hundred percent back to normal. But it was a heck of a lot closer than a month ago.

Nearly everyone was relaxing into the change, and Gray could sense a gradual return to the trust in him he'd once taken for granted.

And he thought *he* had relaxed into the change too. For a long time he'd had no idea he'd even needed to —nor even acknowledged that Gordon's retirement was a major change for him. Not just the people he worked with.

It had been Lanie who'd made him figure that out. Lanie swimming alone in the ocean, working her way through the biggest change in her life with so much dignity—and also moments of weakness.

Those moments were okay, though. Necessary, even.

So he too was allowing himself to be less than perfect. To adjust. To—as Lanie had told him—accept that he could do no more than his best.

It was all he and she could ever do. And that was okay.

It appeared to be working, too. This week he'd sold one of the Hoi An villas.

'It's over. With Tasha,' Gordon said out of the blue.

'I'm sorry to hear that,' Gray said, taking a sip of his beer.

'But not surprised?'

Gray shrugged. 'No.'

Normally that was as far as his conversations with his father went in relation to his divorces.

'What happened?' he asked, surprising himself.

Gordon raised his eyebrows, but answered the question. 'It wasn't working,' he said. 'It didn't turn out as either of us had expected.'

'And what *did* you expect?'

His father smiled. 'The perfect marriage, maybe?'

'What's that?'

Now a laugh. 'Maybe that's the problem. I don't know. Not what I keep on getting, anyway.'

'So why keep on trying?'

Gordon put down his beer glass as he studied Gray. 'I don't know. Each time it seems like a good idea. The best idea, even.'

'It's a good thing you're better at learning from your mistakes in other areas of your life,' Gray pointed out.

'Ah,' Gordon said. 'That's the thing, Gray. I married seven very different women. Given I didn't marry any of them twice, you could say I *did* learn.'

Gray laughed.

Their conversation shifted to more familiar territory—business, mostly. But Gray found himself studying his father and trying to understand how he was feeling.

Because surely—given he'd just separated from a woman he'd supposedly loved—there should be some evidence of... he didn't know... Hurt? Anger? Sadness?

He'd never been able to relate before. When his father had announced his separations—the ones Gray could remember, anyway—he'd paid little attention. As his dad said, Gray had always expected the demise of each relationship. It had never been a surprise.

He'd felt a little smug, actually, that once again he'd been proved right.

But this time he felt ashamed of his previous behaviour. His father must be devastated to have lost such a connection with another person. To have lost that spark, that magic, a person to share your day with. To laugh with. To share *everything* with.

And yet as his father related some golfing anecdote Gray didn't see any of that. No sadness. No regret. Nothing.

'Did you love her?' he asked, interrupting his father.

The older man's eyes widened. 'I thought I did,' he said, after a long moment. 'But no. I didn't. If I had, I don't think I'd feel so relieved that it's over.'

Yes, that was it. *Relief.* That was his dad's overriding emotion. As it had been in every divorce that Gray could remember.

Relief. Wasn't that what he should be feeling when it came to Lanie?

She'd done the right thing by ending it. She'd been absolutely right. Their relationship hadn't been going anywhere.

And, more importantly, she *did* deserve more than that. A lot more than that.

She deserved everything she'd spoken about that night—to live her life beyond her swimming career and to fill it with experiences, and joy, and definitely with love.

In which case, why was he thinking about her now?

Now, weeks later—weeks since he'd seen her, given he'd

changed his daily running track. He'd figured it wouldn't be fair to Lanie to share her beach.

Or fair to him…

He went to take another long drink of his beer—only to realise his glass was empty.

He had no idea what his father was saying, but he nodded occasionally as he tried to pull his own thoughts together.

He did know one thing: he *wasn't* relieved that things had ended with Lanie.

Lanie sighed as she unknotted her apron and hung it on a hook in the café's small office.

Bob grinned as he looked up from counting the day's takings. 'You'll get used to it.'

She smiled back. 'Honestly, you'd think after all my years of swimming I'd be fit enough to run about all day.'

'Maybe that should be your plan when you reopen the place—an underwater café. Then you could swim the orders out to customers.'

Lanie tilted her head, as if giving the idea serious consideration. 'You know, you could be onto something.'

Five minutes later, with her bag swung over her shoulder, she headed for the beach. The little café shut each day at five p.m.—something she *did* plan to change when her purchase of the café was finalised—and at this time of year there were still hours of daylight remaining.

The sand was only sparsely dotted with people—a few sunbathers, a handful of dogs, and some kids splashing about in the shallows. The afternoon sea breeze had kicked in, and it urged small white-tipped waves from the ocean. One hopeful surfer bobbed just behind the waves, and far, far beyond him a lone container ship was silhouetted against the sky.

Lanie dumped her bag, quickly tugged her cotton dress off over her bathers, then pulled her swim-cap on over her hair. Lacing her fingers behind her back, she stretched her shoulders and chest slowly, then moved through the remainder of her stretching routine. She finished by sitting on her towel, her fingers wrapped around her feet as she pulled them gently towards herself to stretch the muscles of her hips and legs.

Now was normally the point when she leapt to her feet—ready and raring to go, to feel the shocking coolness of the ocean against her skin, and then minutes later the satisfying burn in her lungs.

But today she paused.

The sun was still high in the sky, and it made her squint as she stared out to the horizon.

She should be feeling good. Fantastic, even.

The moment Bob had told her he was retiring and selling his business she'd known taking over the café and his lease on the building was the right thing for her to do. It had taken every cent of her savings, plus a substantial loan, but she figured her own home could wait, and for now she was living in the two tiny rooms at the back of the café.

Lanie now knew she couldn't work for anyone but herself—and not just because of her experience working with Gray. She needed to feel in complete control of this next phase of her life—good or bad, *she* was in charge of what happened next. That meant a lot to her.

But this was going to be good. She truly believed it—especially when she was down here at the beach.

This place reassured her.

Here she was in her element. The ocean didn't think she was tall or awkward—in fact amongst the waves she felt alive, strong, powerful. Elegant in a way she'd never felt in a fifty-metre pool. There she'd compared herself to others—to the girls on the blocks either side of her, to her sister.

Someone was always faster, prettier, or more talented.

But here in the ocean she let go of all that. She stopped judging herself. Stopped judging others.

It was impossible not to—out there it was just her in the water. No stopwatches, no competitors, no finish line.

In the water sometimes she even felt beautiful.

She never had before—except, of course, with Gray.

She shook her legs as if to chase the memories of Gray away.

There was absolutely no point thinking of him, although knowing that didn't really stop it happening. Especially when she swam.

Lanie clambered to her feet and slid her goggles over her eyes.

Stroke, stroke, stroke, *breathe.*

The sun was about to start moving towards the horizon as Lanie swam towards the shore. She pulled her cap and goggles off and held them in one hand as she dived beneath the surface, finger-combing her tangled hair away from her face.

Moments later a splash a few metres to her left grabbed her attention. A tennis ball, bright yellow, bobbed beside her.

Its owner made himself apparent almost immediately, leaping through the water until his paws didn't reach the bottom, then thrashing about enthusiastically as he paddled to the ball.

Luther.

True to form, the dog ignored her entirely, his focus exclusively on his prized possession. He snatched the ball up into his mouth, then swiftly made his way back to the sand—only to drop the ball as soon as he got there, then look back at Lanie, his body tense with anticipation.

'I can't throw it from out here, mate.'

A male voice—Gray's voice—immediately to her right.

As if the dog understood he happily trotted a few metres up the beach, then dropped to his stomach, the ball between his paws. Waiting patiently.

Of course Gray was here, if Luther was. But still, having him so close was unexpected and disconcerting. Or at least that was the reason she gave for the way her tummy immediately lightened at the familiar sound of his voice.

She'd been swimming back, but now the water was shallow enough to stand, so she did as she turned to face Gray. He was standing in the water too, his hair slicked back and his bare chest gleaming in the sun.

'Hey,' he said.

'Hi.'

For long minutes they just stood there. Lanie didn't know what to do or to say.

'Bob told me you bought his café,' Gray said eventually.

She nodded. 'Yeah. He's spent the past month teaching me everything he knows, and then he's leaving me to it.'

'You'll do great.'

'That's the plan.'

The terribly awkward conversation segued into an even more awkward silence. Lanie realised she was still splashing her cap and goggles about in the water, so she made her hands go still.

'I'm glad you came back to the beach. Luther loves it here. I hope you weren't avoiding it because of me,' she said. Her gaze drifted to the shore and she wished herself back at her towel. Or at home. Anywhere but here.

Because it had been bad enough thinking about Gray over the past few weeks. Standing metres away from him was impossible.

'Of course I was avoiding it because of you.'

Her attention snapped back to Gray. 'Oh,' she said. 'You shouldn't.'

'Why not?'

She attempted a blasé laugh. 'I'd hate for one simple weekend to ruin North Cottesloe beach for you for ever. Seems a bit dramatic, don't you think?'

'But that was the problem, wasn't it, Lanie? It was more than just a weekend.'

Lanie's realised she was gripping her goggles so hard that they were digging into her palms.

'You didn't seem to think so,' she said, then immediately wished the words back.

She needed to end this conversation now. It was pointless. They'd covered all this before. And it hurt just as much the second time around.

'What if I was wrong?'

She made herself meet his gaze, trying to ignore the pathetic butterflies of hope that swirled around her stomach. 'Were you?'

He nodded. 'I used to think that love was a weakness. A possible chink in my armour. A risk—a complication that I didn't need and that could distract me and shift my focus from what was really important.'

'Which is Manning,' she said.

He shook his head. 'No. It's part of it—but now I know it's not everything. It's not even close to everything I need in my life. My dad knows that too. That's why he keeps searching for love. He definitely doesn't always make the right decisions, but I can no longer deride him for trying. We've been talking a lot, and I think once he was in love. He keeps searching for that feeling again.'

Gray had stepped closer—or maybe the waves had pushed them closer together.

His gaze was still locked with hers, and he was now near enough that she could see the intensity in his eyes. And she could certainly feel it. Right now she had no doubt she was all he was seeing.

Maybe right now she was all that mattered.

It was an overwhelming sensation. But it drew her towards him like a magnet.

Another step through the lapping waves. So that if she reached out she could touch him.

'I don't want to be like him,' Gray said. 'I don't want to spend the rest of my life searching for something I once had.'

'Or getting married seven times?'

He laughed out loud. 'I can't see that happening.'

No, but Lanie could too easily imagine Gray shutting himself off from the world, keeping his distance in the guise of arrogance.

Gray took that last final step. The step that made her tilt her chin up to look at him and made each deep breath she took bring their bodies dangerously close together.

'I love you, Lanie,' he said.

After everything, it seemed almost too simple. Too basic and straightforward when everything about their relationship had been complicated and confusing.

But it was far from simple.

Could she do this? Could she risk herself again? Could she risk the all too familiar pain of rejection and failure?

The possibility scared her. Terrified her, even.

But as she looked up into Gray's eyes she didn't see any doubts.

And when she searched inside herself she couldn't find any either.

She wouldn't take back a moment of her swimming career, even though it hadn't ended the way she'd dreamed.

Besides, this was love—not sport.

Sure, there were risks, and no guarantees.

But their love wasn't dependent on others. On injury, or illness, or team selection policy.

It was just her and Gray.

'I love you, too,' she said softly, just loud enough to be heard over the gentle splash of the ocean.

Then she was in his arms and kissing him, with the taste of salt water on her lips and the bite of the sun warm against their damp skin.

On the beach, Luther barked—loudly.

It took a while, but eventually they broke apart.

'I think he wants someone to throw his ball,' Lanie said, smiling.

And, hand in hand, they walked back to the shore, together.

* * * * *

Mills & Boon® Hardback

December 2013

ROMANCE

MEDICAL

ROMANCE

HISTORICAL

MEDICAL

Mills & Boon® Hardback

January 2014

ROMANCE

The Dimitrakos Proposition	Lynne Graham
His Temporary Mistress	Cathy Williams
A Man Without Mercy	Miranda Lee
The Flaw in His Diamond	Susan Stephens
Forged in the Desert Heat	Maisey Yates
The Tycoon's Delicious Distraction	Maggie Cox
A Deal with Benefits	Susanna Carr
The Most Expensive Lie of All	Michelle Conder
The Dance Off	Ally Blake
Confessions of a Bad Bridesmaid	Jennifer Rae
The Greek's Tiny Miracle	Rebecca Winters
The Man Behind the Mask	Barbara Wallace
English Girl in New York	Scarlet Wilson
The Final Falcon Says I Do	Lucy Gordon
Mr (Not Quite) Perfect	Jessica Hart
After the Party	Jackie Braun
Her Hard to Resist Husband	Tina Beckett
Mr Right All Along	Jennifer Taylor

MEDICAL

The Rebel Doc Who Stole Her Heart	Susan Carlisle
From Duty to Daddy	Sue MacKay
Changed by His Son's Smile	Robin Gianna
Her Miracle Twins	Margaret Barker

Mills & Boon® Large Print

January 2014

ROMANCE

Challenging Dante	Lynne Graham
Captivated by Her Innocence	Kim Lawrence
Lost to the Desert Warrior	Sarah Morgan
His Unexpected Legacy	Chantelle Shaw
Never Say No to a Caffarelli	Melanie Milburne
His Ring Is Not Enough	Maisey Yates
A Reputation to Uphold	Victoria Parker
Bound by a Baby	Kate Hardy
In the Line of Duty	Ami Weaver
Patchwork Family in the Outback	Soraya Lane
The Rebound Guy	Fiona Harper

HISTORICAL

Mistress at Midnight	Sophia James
The Runaway Countess	Amanda McCabe
In the Commodore's Hands	Mary Nichols
Promised to the Crusader	Anne Herries
Beauty and the Baron	Deborah Hale

MEDICAL

Dr Dark and Far-Too Delicious	Carol Marinelli
Secrets of a Career Girl	Carol Marinelli
The Gift of a Child	Sue MacKay
How to Resist a Heartbreaker	Louisa George
A Date with the Ice Princess	Kate Hardy
The Rebel Who Loved Her	Jennifer Taylor